Sleep Tight, Mr. Carter!

It was four in the morning, the dead hour, when a normal man's reactions were slowest and his sleep was the deepest.

But Carter hadn't survived for years in the killing business by being a normal man. The instant the rhythm of sound changed, his eyes popped open and his body tensed.

What was it? A click, and then a slight scrape. He rolled his eyes to the open glass doors leading to the balcony. Suddenly a hulk blotted out the moon and Carter rolled to the floor.

The click he had heard was the safety of a gun being released. The two dull pops, like champagne corks being softly released from a bottle, were unmistakable. He didn't have to look to know that right now, two slugs were embedded in the mattress where, seconds before, he had been sleeping . . .

NICK CARTER IS IT!

FROM THE NICK CARTER
KILLMASTER SERIES

HOLIDAY IN HELL

KILL MASTER

NICK CARTER

J
JOVE BOOKS, NEW YORK

KILLMASTER #251: HOLIDAY IN HELL

A Jove Book / published by arrangement with
The Condé Nast Publications, Inc.

PRINTING HISTORY
Jove edition / July 1989

ISBN: 0-515-10060-9

Jove Books are published by The Berkley Publishing Group,
200 Madison Avenue, New York, New York 10016.
The name "JOVE" and the "J" logo
are trademarks belonging to Jove Publications, Inc.

PRINTED IN THE UNITED STATES OF AMERICA

10 9 8 7 6 5 4 3 2 1

*Dedicated to the men and women of the
Secret Services of the
United States of America*

ONE

It was nearly midnight when Senator Samuel Lloyd stepped from the New York–Washington shuttle and merged with the crowd surging toward the terminal exits.

Lloyd walked erect, making himself appear taller than his five feet nine. He was a slender man who prided himself on keeping his weight within five pounds of what it had been when he graduated from law school thirty years earlier.

His silver-gray hair framed his face majestically, each one of those hairs carefully attended to by the Senate barber every Wednesday morning at nine sharp.

As he walked, a briefcase swung in his right hand with almost military precision. With the fingers of his left hand he smoothed his silver mustache and slitted his cold green eyes. He was a good-looking man for his age, and he took great care with his appearance. Impressions were very important to a man like Lloyd. Even now, in the middle of the night, he wore a brown tweed suit with belted jacket and sharply creased trousers that broke just so over hand-made, mahogany-hued half-boots.

1

Only his closest intimates would realize that Lloyd was dead tired. It had been one hell of a week. It was Thursday, and since Monday he had been waging his own private lobbying war at the U.N.

At the glass doors, he peered through the swirling snow, knowing she wouldn't be there. He had told her he would be back on Friday night. Coming back a day early had come from pure weariness.

He made his way to the long line of taxis.

"Where to, sir?"

"Watergate," Lloyd replied, passing over his carryon bag. Declining to surrender his briefcase, he crawled wearily into the back seat of the taxi.

"Which entrance, sir?"

"The east side," he muttered, and the driver rolled the cab out toward the Jeff Davis Highway. Fog lights barely cut through the swirling snow, which had been preceded by rain and sleet.

"This is gonna be hell when it freezes," the driver commented.

Lloyd only grunted. His mind was on a hot shower, a soft bed, and the even softer body of his youthful wife.

By hunching his shoulders and slouching into the seat, he blotted out the lights and the traffic sounds. He wanted a cigarette, but he was too tired to move. He dozed until the cab stopped.

He paid the driver and took the elevator to his floor. There was no sound on the other side of the door. That was odd. Generally, when he was away, she stayed up half the night watching television.

He let himself in with his key and gently closed the door behind him.

For some reason—if reason functions at the instinctual level—he didn't turn on the hall light. Instead he stood transfixed in the dark, hardly breathing, suddenly alerted. And the close-cropped hairs at the back of his neck seemed to tingle.

He could hear muted voices, which at first he thought might be coming from the television.

Then he heard her laugh—modulated, cultivated—so low. He kicked open the door and snapped on the switch, flooding the bedroom in light.

"Jesus . . ."

At the sound of his voice the young man rolled off her body. Joanna sat up, her unfettered breasts dancing. She made no move to cover any part of her naked body.

"Darling," she said lightly, "you're home early."

"So it would appear," Lloyd said flatly. "And you're up late. At your age, you shouldn't deprive yourself of your beauty sleep." He nodded his head slightly. "Somebody ought to introduce us."

By that time the young man was scrambling into his trousers, and his bare feet shuffled for the loafers beside the bed.

"I . . . I . . ." the boy stuttered.

"Never mind," Lloyd sighed. "Just get the hell out and forget you were here."

"Yes, sir . . . yes, sir." The young man's big, limpid brown eyes were full of fear.

Lloyd's eyes flicked to his wife's face. Her eyes actually looked sad, but there was a smile still fluttering around her lips.

Somehow it infuriated him. As the young man tried to scoot past him toward the door, Lloyd let go his fury.

Mechanically, with an economy of motion, Lloyd stepped forward and slammed a knee into the boy's groin. Both he and Joanna screamed. As the young man doubled over in pain, retching, Lloyd backhanded him against the wall.

"I . . . I can't fight you, please," the young man gasped.

"Fine, then I won't hit you too hard," Lloyd said agreeably.

This time he lashed out with the heel of his right hand and separated several of the boy's front teeth from his gums.

"Sam!" Joanna cried. "For the love of God!"

"Not at all," Lloyd said. "It's not even for the love of you."

The boy, on his knees now and gagging, could only gasp, "Please, please . . ."

"He'll be all right," Lloyd said. "I think he may have swallowed a tooth." Then he stepped forward and kicked him in the ribs. "Get out of here, kid. If I ever catch you around here again, I'll kill you. You can count on that. Now get going."

Gasping and gagging, the young man dragged himself to the door. He was bent far forward, clutching his unzipped trousers with one hand, dragging his suit jacket with the other. He stumbled from the apartment without another word.

Lloyd followed him to the entrance hall to close the front door. Joanna had recovered her aplomb when he returned.

"He'll freeze," she said quietly. "He forgot his coat."

"Then he'll just have to freeze, Joanna. Everybody has to face the consequences of his actions in this world —him, you, me."

As Lloyd undressed, his wife crawled from the bed. Naked, she folded her arms as if to shield herself from his view until she fumbled into a robe.

"I'm sorry," she murmured.

"Sure," he replied dryly.

"I told you, promised you, it wouldn't happen again, I know. . ."

"But it did."

"I couldn't help myself."

"Tell you what, Joanna—I don't want to talk about it anymore."

He left the bedroom, went across the large apartment into his study, and turned on the desk lamp.

He fixed himself a drink, putting a couple of ice cubes in a tumbler then filling the glass with scotch. Some of the whiskey sloshed over the side of the full glass as he eased himself into a big leather chair. For a long time he just sat there. Then he drank the scotch straight back.

He was so tired he couldn't actually decide whether he had slept or entered a kind of shock trance. When he next looked at his watch it was four o'clock in the morning. The cigarette had burned a little hole in the rug. He was very cold and his face was damp with tears.

It was nearly dawn when he opened his eyes again and saw her standing, posed, in front of his chair.

The robe she wore was like a lens filter over the glory of her body. Every curve and hollow, every shade of color, was clear to his tortured eyes.

Her breasts, heavy yet firm and high, were creamy white and tipped with dark points like huge dark mounds of enticing lust. Her shoulders were firm, yet capable of turning to melted butter when the right man put his arms around them. Her ribs poked excitingly against the flawless skin below her breasts, pointing like arrows to her navel. The sweet indentation of her belly button was set in the taut pillow of her belly. It led the way to her crotch, where, somewhere under that darkness, all her passion sat now in seething silence.

"I think I should go away," she said quietly.

"You want to leave me?" he asked.

"No, just go away for a while. A holiday, until whatever you're going through is over."

"The Namibia question."

She shrugged. "If that's what is wrong, then the Namibia question. You said it would be settled in a couple of weeks. I'll go away until then."

"I'm sorry I hit the boy."

She laughed lightly. "I just wish you had so much volatility in bed."

Lloyd winced. He was fifty-eight. She was twenty-six. His friends on the Hill had said such a May-September marriage would never work.

But he loved her. God, how he loved her.

"I'm sorry," she said, dropping on her knees before him. "That was out of line."

He moved his hands to her shoulders and down her back. "You know I forgive you."

"I know."

"I always have. I always will."

"I know, Sam."

Muscle by muscle he forced himself to relax, then with his eyes boring into hers, he swung in the chair. But instead of facing away, he faced her, running his hands up the backs of her thighs, cupping her buttocks and pulling her close. He pressed his face into the warm pillows of her breasts, but immediately she pushed his shoulders back, gaining her freedom.

"Not yet. I feel feminine and powerful when I make you wait. Relax . . . close your eyes . . . please."

He did. And stopped trying to claim her, resting his wrists on the chair, letting his relaxed fingers trail toward the floor. His shoulders slumped a little. His head relaxed and his lips parted slightly. Though his breathing was still pressured, the rest of him waited in apparent repose.

"Where would you go?"

"Greece," she replied, stroking his face with the tips of her fingers. "Remember your friend, Chandra Braxton, invited us to cruise with her on her yacht?"

"Yes."

"I know you can't go, but I could. And you wouldn't have to fear, Sam. She would be my chaperone. I wouldn't be in your hair while you're trying to get this Namibia bill passed, and she would be there to make sure I didn't embarrass you."

He blinked, his body shuddered, and his hands shook. What she said was true. If he didn't have to worry about her, he could get the Namibia question settled. That one piece of legislation would ensure his re-election.

"Well, Sam?"

He nodded. "I'll call Chandra in the morning and make the arrangements."

This time she let his hands explore her body. Slowly she worked him into the bedroom and to the bed.

He stretched out and she gently undressed him. When he was naked, she massaged the stiffness from the muscles in his neck and shoulders.

She knew him well. In a matter of minutes he was sound asleep.

Joanna padded back to the study, picked up the phone, and dialed a local Washington number.

"Yes?"

"I am a go, day after tomorrow."

"Greece?"

"Yes. The boy, Spider?"

"He will be taken care of."

"*Ciao.*"

She hung up and walked to the guest bathroom. There she took a long shower to wash the seed of the boy and the touch of her husband from her body.

Spider Fry was scared to death. He finished dressing in the elevator down to the east exit.

Jesus, he thought, sprinting to his car, *an easy pickup, a quick piece, and her old man shows up*.

Not once in the two nights she had come on to him in the club had she said she was married. But what the hell, most of them were married . . . and old.

This one was different. She was young, not more than four or five years older than he was.

Hell, he would have laid up with this one for a hell of a lot less than the hundred she offered. Hell, he would have screwed the hell out of this one for nothing.

Crazy. Nuts. Weird.

And he hadn't even gotten the hundred. All he'd gotten was busted balls and teeth and maybe a broken collarbone. No doubt about it. He had to get into a different line of work. Now he saw why most female strippers didn't like men. Spider was a male stripper, and he was beginning to go sour on women.

He drove south to the Beltway and then east toward Maryland. He dropped off the parkway at Laurel, made all three stoplights, and pulled up in the rear of his apartment house.

He parked the Camaro and walked across the narrow lot to the gate that led into the pool area.

Spider never made it. They were shadows, coming out of the shadows of the tall shrubbery by the chain link fence.

He made one small sound as a fist crashed into his stomach, knocking the breath out of him. While he was doubled over with pain, another fist struck him in the face and broke his nose. The big rectangular setting in a signet ring slashed his upper lip as cleanly as a razor.

Spider felt blood streaming down his neck. A kick caught him in the stomach. A sharp pain started from his side and spread to the tips of his fingers and toes. He fell.

A heel crushed his left cheek. He heard something snap in his jaw but felt no pain.

The two men picked him up by pulling on his wrists. One of them drew back his head by the hair, exposing his throat. A fist hit him on the Adam's apple. He felt as if he were shrinking like a deflated balloon.

Another fist hit him even harder on the left eye, which was already swollen shut.

Even as Spider fell to the cold asphalt, he somehow knew he was going to die.

TWO

Nick Carter stepped from the cab and pulled the collar of his overcoat up to shield his neck against the thick flakes of snow that swirled in cold funnels around him.

Forty-eight hours ago it had been snowing when he left Washington. It had caught up with him twenty-four hours later in Zurich. Now, in Berlin, it was still with him.

He looked up at the façade of the Schweizerhof Hotel. It was a good choice, expensive and Swiss-owned. It was just the right hotel for a successful Swiss banker to stay in when he was on an expense-paid junket to Berlin.

His eyes peered through the snow to the double doors of tinted glass and beyond to the sumptuously appointed lobby. It looked warm and inviting.

But that wasn't what interested the Killmaster from AXE. He was casing the loungers in the lobby, the people moving in and out of the doors, looking for one he recognized or one who recognized him.

Hawk's word: "He's a double, Nick, code-named

10

Butterfly. If he suspects, he may well try to take you out even before you get into East Berlin."

Carter saw no one who might be watching for his arrival as he followed the porter and his bag up the stairs and into the lobby.

Inside the hotel, warm air quickly melted the snow from his dark hair and wide shoulders. He let the porter who'd taken his suitcase from the cab go to the registration desk at a brisk pace.

Carter followed slowly, looking over the lobby. It was a high-ceilinged room, with potted plants in the corners, a large, gold-veined mirror on one wall, and a plush wine-red carpet flowing everywhere. Against the marble walls stood settees modeled after nineteenth-century designs, with ornately carved claw legs, gilt armrests, and huge, rounded cushions on back and seat. They looked extremely uncomfortable, but the few people sitting on them did not. They looked like the kind of people who would be comfortable sitting on anything that cost a lot of money.

None of them showed any interest in Carter.

"Good evening, mein Herr. You have a reservation this evening?" The concierge was a tired little man with a pale face who was probably a CPA in another life and would be again in his next incarnation.

"Yes, a suite," Carter replied in Swiss-Deutsch. "The name is Press, Rudolph Press."

"Of course, sir, Eurobank, Zurich." The concierge busied himself with registration cards, passport, and general busywork.

Carter took another casual glance around the lobby. Not a single person had a bulge in his coat he shouldn't have had, or paid him the slightest bit of attention.

Carter felt most of the tension he had been feeling drain from his body.

He registered, signed the fictitious name to the pay voucher, and picked up his passport.

"If your stay will be longer than a week, Herr Press, please inform us?"

If my stay is longer than two nights it will be too long.

"I'll do that," Carter replied, moving along after the bellman and his bag.

The bellman pushed the button marked eight. The doors opened. Just as Carter was about to step into the elevator he heard a low, husky, very female voice behind him.

"Nick, what brings you to Berlin?"

At the mention of his real name, hairs prickled on the back of his neck. He forced a blank look on his face and casually turned, as if he were mildly curious to learn who could possess such a beautiful voice and be speaking to him.

Of course he already knew.

Her name was Chandra Braxton. She owned nine or ten posh apartments and houses around the world, a palace on the Greek island of Mykonos, and a floating palace called the *Noble Savage*.

Besides being one of the biggest arms manufacturers and brokers in the world, Chandra Braxton was also mature and voluptuously beautiful.

Now, staring up at him, a puzzled frown furrowing her brow, he thought she had never looked more beautiful. Her hair was short, as he remembered it, and dark with twin streaks of gray at the sides, flowing back over her ears. Deep green eyes stared from an almost but not quite classical face. The mouth was a little too full and the nose a little too large. Her beauty was harsh, slightly cold, like its owner.

She was dressed in a strapless black gown. The material flowed over her lush figure like a barely moving mountain stream. Her only jewelry was a few thousand dollars' worth of diamonds at her throat and wrists. An ankle-length sable coat was thrown casually over her bare shoulders.

"Nick," she said, "it's been at least a year. How are you?"

"I am sorry," he replied, "I am afraid I don't speak English very well."

She opened her mouth as if to disagree, and then read the stark warning in Carter's eyes. She darted a glance toward the bellman and then the key in his hand.

She closed her mouth slowly, then smiled as though embarrassed.

"I am terribly sorry," she murmured, "I thought you were an old friend."

Carter smiled, clicked his heels, and gave her a nodding bow. "Fräulein, I wish I were."

She gave him a cold smile and a nod. "Forgive me."

Carter watched her turn and walk like a queen toward the front doors. He stared after her for a moment and then, with a sigh, got into the elevator.

"You were almost a very lucky man, mein Herr," the bellman said, chuckling.

"*Ja, ja,*" Carter said, nodding, "but what would my wife say?"

He tipped the bellman well. As soon as the door closed behind the man, he went through the suite. He knew it wasn't necessary, but habit was hard to break and caution meant survival.

He looked under the furniture, behind an expensively framed painting, in the television console, and in the light fixtures. He found nothing that shouldn't have been there in the room. When he had finished his search, he opened the false bottom of his bag and took

out a 9mm Luger. From the same place he withdrew a
roll of adhesive tape.

He pulled a heavy night table by the bed away from
the wall and sat on the bed. Carefully, he taped the
Luger to the back of the table, then replaced it far
enough from the wall so he could get to it quickly.

This done, he peeled off his clothes and stood for ten
minutes under an alternating hot and cold shower.
Mostly dry, he wrapped the towel around his middle and
moved into the sitting room and the mini-bar. With
three fingers of Chivas in a glass, he headed back to the
bedroom and the television.

He had just flipped it on, when there was a knock at
the door.

One frozen second. He left the television on, sound
off, and slid the Luger from the taped holster. Shutting
off all the lights, he moved back to the door.

"Ja?"

The knocking was repeated.

"Wer sind sie, bitte?"

A raspy voice, muted by the solid door: "It's me.
Open up, Nick."

Silently, he unlocked the door and moved to a corner.
He trained his Luger on the center of the door and
flipped the safety off.

"Kommen sie herien."

She held the door open, staring into the darkness,
then reached for the light switch.

Carter's steel tone stopped her. "I like it dark. Step
in. Close the door, lock it."

"Christ, Nick . . ."

"Do it!"

She did as he said, then leaned her back against the
door, her hands behind her. Carter turned on a lamp.

"You really know how to make a lady welcome," she murmured, "and I don't mean the towel."

"You're not welcome."

Anger flashed in her eyes. "Screw you, buster." She whirled and reached for the lock.

Carter caught her wrist. "Chandra . . . I'm on a job."

She turned to face him, her eyes wide. Only then did she seem to notice the Luger. "Oh, shit, Nick, I'm sorry. Did I screw you up?"

He shrugged. "Probably not. I'm just touchy. It's that kind of a job."

"Should I disappear?"

"Anyone see you in the hall, knocking on my door?"

"No . . . no, I'm sure of it."

He put the safety on and tossed the Luger on the bed. "Then it should be all right."

She pushed away from the door and moved to him. She stopped in front of him and leaned her breasts against his bare chest like a pagan offering. Her pink tongue licked across her lips, wetting them and making them glisten.

"The least you can do is repay the lady's hospitality. If you remember, you lived on my yacht—and in my bed—for a month."

Carter smiled. "Oh, I remember."

He looked down into the woman's eyes when he felt her arms snake under his and around behind him. Her fingers ran along his spine. She went up on tiptoes and brushed his mouth with her wet lips. He responded to her, slowly, reluctantly, in spite of himself.

After a moment she stepped back and looked at him, as if to admire her handiwork. She saw the yearning in his eyes, and she half smiled, satisfied, as though she had seen proof of her competence.

"Got anything to drink in this dump?" she asked with a smile.

Carter coughed. "One drink coming up."

He got his own drink and built her one. She dropped the sable casually on the floor and curled up on the sofa with her legs under her. The black dress rode to mid-thigh and she didn't bother pulling it down.

"What brings you to Berlin, especially in winter?" he asked, handing her the drink.

"All business, but I finished it this afternoon. Tonight was a little party. I leave in the morning."

Carter couldn't keep the relief out of his eyes. Over the rim of her glass she caught it.

"Won't they miss you at the party?"

"They'll survive," she answered, shrugging her bare shoulders.

"What was the business?"

Her green eyes flashed for an instant. "What the hell is this, a third degree?"

Carter sighed. He moved from the chair to the sofa beside her. "Chandra, I'm in the fire. Nothing goes down until tomorrow night, but maybe, just maybe, you could get a little burned being around me."

She smiled and her tongue came out to lick the rim of the glass. "I was there before."

"Yeah, you were."

And she had been. It had been a mess in the little African country of Togo. A huge conglomerate had eyes to take over the country with the help of a greedy dictator. Chandra Braxton's smarts and wealth had been one of the major reasons they hadn't pulled it off.

When the mess had been cleaned up, Carter had taken a long holiday aboard her yacht, the *Noble Savage*.

It was one hell of a month.

"You're reminiscing," she teased.

"Yeah, a month of balmy Greek nights."

She threw her head back and laughed, showing the fine lines at her throat. Carter looked at her throat and then lower, at the top of her dress where her breasts were fighting for freedom.

"It's been a long time," he said.

"Too long. C'mere."

He went, willingly. She touched his chest, his shoulders, then moved her fingers down his arms. He kissed her and her lips parted, allowing his tongue to slip into her warm, receptive mouth. He could feel her body begin to tremble as she brought her tongue forward and made contact with his. She could feel the hardness under his towel as his hand slipped inside the dress and found her breast, the nipple already taut with excitement.

He stood and pulled her to her feet. Her hands tugged and the towel fell to the floor.

She looked down. "My, my, it has been a long time."

"And I've got a long memory."

He reached for the zipper on her dress, listened to it purr down her back. She wiggled the dress off her hips and let it slide to the floor.

She wore nothing beneath it.

"Do you always run around with no underwear?"

She chuckled. "Panties and pantyhose. They're in my purse. Took 'em off in the elevator."

"Chandra Braxton, you are the most wanton old woman I know."

"Wanton, yes. Mention my age and you can take care of this yourself."

She squeezed him but it was far from painful.

He touched her naked flesh at the base of her back, kneaded it gently, and she pressed herself to him.

"Kiss me."

He did, long and deep. Her breathing was heavy as their lips parted and he kissed her neck and nibbled at her ear. When his mouth found its way down to her breast and engulfed one nipple, she moaned.

Carter kept his mouth busy on her thrusting breast and reached around and grasped her taut buttocks. She straddled one of his legs and massaged her sex against his muscular thigh. Her hand slipped down and her fingers fondled the length of his erection.

"Guess what?"

"What?" he groaned.

"I think the preliminaries are over."

She wrapped her arms tightly around his neck as he carried her into the bedroom. Together they fell to the bed.

The look in his eyes as he stared at her breasts was one of naked desire. Her nipples were erect. With a groan he buried his head between them, bathing the skin of the shadowed valley with his tongue. Her hands caressed his head and the nape of his neck, her fingers flickering lightly over his back and shoulders.

His mouth went to the other nipple and showered it with kisses. Then his lips closed over the tip. She moaned. Her nipples were turgid. She cradled his head on her breast.

"I love it," she purred.

The next moment he was inside her, all power and strength. She gave a little wordless cry as they began to move in unison. Ever deepening waves of desire washed over them as their intoxication with each other mounted, waves that seemed to break with increasing frequency, until they dissolved together in mutual delight.

• • •

They lay on their backs, side by side, satiated, lazy.

"I'd better go," she whispered.

"I hate to agree," Carter replied, "but I have to."

She slid from the bed and padded into the bathroom. He lit a cigarette and stared out the window. It was snowing harder now. He hoped it would last. It would make the next night's job that much easier.

The shower stopped and she emerged, patting herself dry with an enormous towel.

"You don't have to tell me, but how tough is this one?"

"Very," was his only reply as he crushed the cigarette. "Actually, the worst kind."

"You said tomorrow night." She discarded the towel and tried to make sense out of her crumpled dress. "This is Saturday. Will it be over by Tuesday?"

He shrugged. "With luck it will be over sometime in the wee hours of Monday morning."

"And then?" she said, sitting on the bed and staring down at him.

He smiled. He could read her thinking in her eyes. "Balmy Greek nights?"

She nodded. "I'm having a few guests for a cruise on the *Noble Savage*, just a few days. Beyond Friday we would be all alone."

Carter reached up and traced the outline of her chin with his fingertip. "I'll call you from Athens."

She stood. "I hoped you would."

Then she was gone, only the scent of her perfume remaining in the air.

A vacation, Carter sighed. *God knows I could use one*.

THREE

The snow had turned into a bone-chilling rain. The sky was gray except for heavy black clouds to the west.

Carter shaved, dressed, and repacked the Luger in the false bottom of his bag. In front of the hotel, he grabbed a cab to a restaurant near the bookstore. He ate ham, eggs, cheese, and drank two cups of coffee.

Before leaving the restaurant, he called the special number for Harry Jens. Harry was an old Berlin hand, some said too old. He had been on the Berlin beat so long that he spoke English with a German accent.

"*Ja?*"

"It's me. Are we set?"

"As much as we'll ever be," came the weary reply. "Have you seen the book man?"

"I'm on my way now. What have you got for me?"

"As soon as Pavel is over," Jens replied, "you take the S-1 Bahn out of Friedrichstrasse."

"Got it. 'Bye."

Carter hung up and walked the short block to the bookstore. It was noon sharp. The blinds were pulled, but he could see movement through a crack in one of them.

He rattled the latch and the curtain parted slightly. A bloodshot eye stared at him for a moment and the door opened.

"Come in, hurry."

Carter stepped inside and followed Herman Fieffer into his living quarters in the rear of the shop. Fieffer had been a dealer of used and rare books for twenty-five years. For fifteen of those twenty-five years he had been forging documents for AXE.

"Here are your papers and those of your client."

Carter checked them. He would be going over with the Rudolph Press passport and a regulation visa. Hopefully, he would return under the name of Ames Johnson from Cleveland, Ohio. Pavel's alias was Gerhard Hauptmann, Frankfurt.

Pavel's entry stamp into East Berlin carried the current day's date. Carter's, as Johnson, was stamped for the next morning at nine o'clock.

"Well?"

"Excellent, as usual," Carter said, and shook the old man's hand.

Outside, he turned up his collar, ducked his head into the rain, and walked for several blocks.

The café had dirty windows and smoke poured from the door when he opened it. A group of workers hung over a chessboard, and the bar was two deep with men watching a soccer match on television.

Carter got a beer and settled in a corner that could be seen from the door.

At 12:30 sharp, the Turk, Anton Nomali, strolled in, glanced around, and headed for Carter's table. A hollow smile played on his firm, wide lips, made longer-looking by a mustache whose ends nearly touched the bottom of his jaw on either side.

His lithe, spare body was made for the tight beige pants, the body-hugging black shirt, and the short-waisted jacket he wore. His boots were elaborately stitched, with high heels and narrow toes.

Anton Nomali looked like what he was: a hood. Carter had worked with him in the past, but he had never liked the man. But Nomali was good at what he did. He had at least four mistresses in East Berlin as well as a good handful of contacts in the black market.

"He made contact around ten last night," the Turk said, sliding into the chair opposite Carter.

"And now?"

"My girl has got him in her room. Here's the address. Her name is Bruna."

"And you're sure she can be trusted?"

"Absolutely. I've used her before." He smiled. There was a large gap between his top front teeth. "She likes the good things in life. I get them for her. Meet her at the Odion Café, seven tonight."

Carter nodded. "I'll send him over at ten sharp. You and Jens pick him up on this side. Jens has a picture so you'll recognize him."

"And you?"

"I'll come through Charlie just before midnight with the return rush of the theater crowd."

"Good luck."

Carter stood. "Let's hope I don't need it."

He walked back into the rain, made sure he wasn't followed, and grabbed a cab.

Greta Hommler's flat was in the Spandau section on Ulriken Strasse. Carter had the driver stop a few blocks away, then he walked.

Still no tail, but then, he thought wryly, why put a

tail on him? They were moving him around like a puppet anyway.

The lobby of the building was sterile and utilitarian, as were most of those built quickly after the war. There was no doorman. A young man in a jogging suit and sneakers slouched in one of the sagging chairs, his face half-hidden behind a magazine.

The automatic elevator let Carter off at the third floor. The hall had a dusty scent. He pressed the button of apartment 3B. Chimes rang inside, a safety chain clattered, the door opened, and Greta Hommler gave him a bawdy wink.

"Long time."

She stood squarely in the doorway, one hip out, her melon breasts thrust forward under a white shirt. The gray eyes were larger than he'd remembered, and would have been beautiful except for the dark rings under them. She stepped out for a quick old-friends kiss on the cheek, then led the way into the living room. She was wearing tight pants. There were no telltale bulges where one might expect them. The legs were still extraordinary.

"Pay no attention to this clutter," she said with a wave of her hand.

The room was a confusion of thrift-shop furniture, a day bed, newspapers, magazines, hints of soap and the musky-sweet scent of a woman.

"Wine?"

Carter shook his head. "No time. I should get over there early if possible."

She nodded. "The car is a Volkswagen, dark blue, a Beetle. It's parked in my number in the garage. The keys." She tossed him the ring.

Carter pocketed the keys. "I'll come back over first,

around ten, in the car. I'm sending Pavel over on foot with the opera crowd just before midnight."

Again she nodded. "The Vopo captain has been taken care of. What names do I give him?"

"I'm using Rudolph Press," Carter replied. "Pavel will come over as Gerhard Hauptman."

She frowned in concentration, memorizing the names, and smiled. "Be careful, Nick. I've worked on this one for a year. He's a scared little man. You'll have to give him a lot of reassurance."

"I'll do the best I can."

Again she pecked him on the cheek, and Carter headed for the garage.

Ilya Pavel was a third-level code clerk in the Russian liaison office. With about a year's worth of interrogation in the West, the man might give them enough intelligence to fill a gnat's ass.

He found the car, got it going, and headed for a nearby garage. It would take about an hour for the special squad to make the installation in the heating system. That would leave plenty of time to go through Checkpoint Charlie before evening.

As he drove across the city, he went over it all again in his mind.

Harry Jens, old, used-up, passed over for promotion several times.

Anton Nomali, a Turk who worked for the British and the Americans because they paid the most money for his services.

Greta Hommler, a West German BfV agent who had worked closely with the Americans on missions for the last three years.

CIA and AXE research had recently found a pattern with all three of them: whatever they had a part in, the mission invariably became screwed up.

One of the three was a double. It would be Carter's job tonight to find out which one.

Checkpoint Charlie was composed of remote-controlled barriers with concrete obstacles between them. It was always manned by anywhere from ten to twenty gray-uniformed Vopos. The crossing was also monitored from observation towers along the wall.

People going or coming had their papers thoroughly scrutinized. The process, when everything went well, took about twenty minutes.

Carter followed instructions. He left the car and entered the little blockhouse. It was half full of Turks and foreign tourists, their teeth chattering.

Outside, Vopos were going over the Volkswagen. They checked under the hood, behind and under the seats. One ran a mirror on a long pole under the car.

"Passport and visa."

Carter handed his papers to the young officer with a broad smile. "Winter has come to Berlin."

"Take off your glasses, please."

Carter removed the glasses he didn't need, waited until the man nodded, and put them back on.

"You know about the midnight curfew?"

"I do," Carter said.

"Fill this out. List everything you are bringing in. Change money there. Next."

He filled out the paper, changed a hundred marks, and returned to the car. Slowly he made his way through the obstacles at ten miles an hour.

The red and white barrier was similar to the one on the Western side. It was a steel cylinder about eight inches in diameter, held in place by thick steel rails. Not even a heavy truck could break through it. Once again he had to show his passport.

The Vopo pressed a button and the barrier rose just long enough to let the Volkswagen pass through.

Carter accelerated. He was in East Germany. In the rearview mirror he saw the little sentry box, with an American flag on it, in the middle of Friedrichstrasse just before the wall. It already seemed to belong to another world.

He drove to Unter den Linden and turned right into the broad avenue. At Alexanderplatz, he turned into a smaller street and parked.

For the next two hours he strolled, playing tourist. Vopos were everywhere. They looked as stern as the general populace looked bored. It seemed that all of them were as inured to the cold as they were to the regimentation of their lives.

The cathedral looked deserted, but then it was supposed to look that way. According to propaganda, no one in the East went to church anymore.

Carter entered, walked to one of the front pews, and knelt, bowing his head to his folded arms.

This would be test number one. Harry Jens had set up this contact to provide Carter with a gun.

He heard a soft footstep to the right of the altar. Barely lifting his head, he peered into the darkness. There was silence for several seconds, and then the soft sound of a door opening.

He saw a shadow move across the floor of the nave. Then he made out a motionless human figure against the dark wall.

He was about to speak, when the figure began to shuffle toward him. At first the sound was strange, and then his ears identified the rasp of a stiff-bristled broom on the stones.

The figure, bent, gray-haired, his shoulders stooped with age, came under the glow of the candles.

"Uncle Bruno?" Carter whispered.

"My only nephew is dead," came the reply.

"He died in a good cause," Carter said.

The figure broomed his way up the aisle. Without ever looking at the man, Carter held out his left arm. A thin automatic was slapped into his palm and he slipped it into his belt at the small of his back.

"Your backup, if you need it, is at number Seventeen Kronenstrasse. His name is Argos, a Greek. It will take a week at least, but he can get you back to the other side if all else fails."

"Let's hope I don't need him, Uncle."

"Let us hope so."

The stiff-bristled broom worked its way back to the altar and the old man disappeared.

Carter waited a full five minutes and stood. He withdrew the automatic and took his time going up the aisle. In the vestibule he released the clip. It was fully loaded and the shells were live.

So much, he thought, *for Harry Jens being the double*.

And then he paused. *That is, if I'm not killed between the cathedral and the Odion Café.*

The Odion was in a dull gray building in Schonhauser Allee. It was made even grayer by the clouds that blotted out the last vestiges of the dim sun and the swirling snow. Carter opened the door and stepped into a small room with a counter on one side. The walls were painted a gloomy brown. He was greeted by an old waiter wearing a threadbare jacket and thick hornrimmed glasses.

"You will be eating, mein Herr?"

"Ja," Carter said, glancing around.

He saw the white sheepskin hat above the wooden

partition of one of the booths along the back wall of the restaurant. In other booths were men in gray uniforms, with women. An old coal stove with a twisted pipe gave off feeble heat.

"That booth there," Carter gestured.

"Ja."

The waiter seated him and handed him a menu. Carter studied it for a moment and then looked at the woman under the white hat.

She wore a thick sweater under a sheepskin jacket, and a skirt that barely reached the curve of her buttocks. He saw a delicate profile, blond hair, blue eyes, and slender, muscular legs encased in black nylon.

She glanced up and gave him a tired smile. It was then he saw the wrinkles around her eyes and the dull, dead quality of her pupils.

She looked to be about thirty-five. Carter guessed she was twenty-five.

Hooking in East Berlin was damn hard work.

Carter ordered beer and bratwurst, and before the waiter could leave grasped his elbow. "The lady," he said, "perhaps she would join me for a schnapps?"

The man frowned until Carter pressed a bill into his hand. Then he leered, crossed to the other booth, and whispered in her ear.

She nodded, stood, and slid into the booth across from Carter. "Good evening, mein Herr."

"Good evening."

The drinks came. She spoke again the moment the waiter was gone, but not so quietly that nearby diners couldn't hear.

"What a cold night, mein Herr."

"It's winter," Carter replied with a smile.

"Mein Herr is from the West?" She had a drink-and-cigarette rasp in her voice and an obvious Berlin accent.

"Swiss . . . Zurich."

"Ahhh. To the Swiss."

Carter acknowledged the toast. She pivoted in the booth. Her legs were crossed and her thighs were aggressively molded by her skirt.

Out of the corner of his eye Carter saw two soldiers drink in the view. He looked their way.

Both of them snickered and fell back into a conversation with each other.

Good, Carter thought. The two top points were established in case there were any Stasi informers in the café. He was Swiss, therefore immune and probably had more than a one-day visa. She was a girl trying to supplement her legal income.

"Your name, mein Herr?"

"Press, Rudolph Press."

"I am called Bruna."

Carter's food came. He ate it, making small talk about the weather, Berlin, and the high price of luxuries.

At the appropriate time, she leaned forward and whispered just loud enough for several people to hear, "Perhaps mein Herr would like to see my Berlin by night?"

"I would like that," he replied.

"We must not leave together," she said.

"Of course not."

Five minutes later Carter paid the bill, left a generous tip, and walked back into the snow.

He took up a position a block away by a bus stop. She soon followed. He watched her approach. Twenty yards behind her came a tall figure in a dark stormcoat, the fur collar turned up high against the weather.

Carter let her get a few paces past, and then fell in

behind her. The man in the heavy coat fell in behind him

Bruna didn't seem to notice that he was following her. She kept walking fast, her hands in the pockets of her sheepskin jacket. She crossed the Rathausstrasse, turned a corner, walked two hundred yards along a narrow street, and went into a gray six-story building.

Carter didn't hesitate. He moved into the hallway right behind her. She was waiting for him.

"We're being followed."

"I know," she said. "Give me fifty marks."

He passed the money to her and she went back into the street. The man in the greatcoat was in a doorway across the street. She spoke a few words, passed over the money, and headed back toward Carter.

By the time she hit the door the man had faded into the snow.

"Stasi?" Carter asked.

She nodded. "He wouldn't have followed us if you had been a Berliner. But Swiss?" She shrugged. "They know you're all rich."

Carter chuckled. "How much would it have cost if I had been a German and he had followed us?"

"Ten marks at the most."

He followed her up the stairs.

The second-story landing appeared. Empty. On the third floor there was a smell of cabbage soup and the sound of a radio news broadcast from the West. The fourth-floor landing was also empty.

On the fifth floor she fumbled a key from her purse. She knocked rapidly and then used the key.

Just before opening the door, she spoke to Carter. "I will be glad when you take this worm off my hands. The little pig hasn't kept his hands off me since I picked him up. He thinks my body comes with the deal."

Carter followed her into the apartment. It was two tiny rooms furnished with castoffs.

"Bruna, Bruna, is that you?"

"Yes, you old fool. Your savior is here."

Ilya Pavel emerged from the darkness of the bedroom. He was a short, thin, stoop-shouldered man with a pinched face and wild eyes. He wore a heavy wool coat and a scarf even though the apartment was hot.

"He's all yours," Bruna said, crossing into the bedroom and slamming the door behind her.

"Whore," Pavel growled. "They didn't tell me that I would have to associate with a common tramp."

Carter sighed as he watched the man take a bottle from his pocket and upend it to his lips. He let the man's Adam's apple bounce three times before he grabbed it out of his hands.

"That's enough."

"Give me that! I've a right—"

Carter pushed him into a chair. "Relax, Pavel. We have about three hours. In that time I have to talk you through every step you're going to take."

The man cursed Carter, groused some more, but he remained in the chair.

"All right, what did you bring me?" Carter asked.

He took a manila folder from beneath the coat and passed it to Carter. Inside was a thick sheaf of papers. The Killmaster went over them line by line for the next hour while Pavel sat and bitched.

It was just as Carter had suspected. There was very little in the papers that was new or that they couldn't have gotten in an easier, much less dangerous way than sending a man into East Berlin.

He glanced up at the other man, his eyes narrowed. "Tell me, Pavel, why did you insist on me as your contact?"

Pavel shrugged. "Your file, in the KGB. You are the best. I didn't want to entrust my life to anyone who wasn't the best."

Carter kept after him for an hour, poking, probing. At the end of that time he was pretty sure he had the answer, as well as the identity of the double.

There has been on old rule of protocol in existence for several years between the KGB and the Western intelligence services: We lie, we steal, we cheat, we even kill. But not each other. It gets too expensive.

They kill one of ours, we kill one of theirs. In the old days it went on all the time and it was counterproductive.

Eventually it became a tacit agreement: hands off in the field, no wet work.

That is, in neutral territory.

But Carter wasn't in neutral territory now. He was on their home ground, East Berlin.

Pavel was bait . . . bait to get him on their home ground.

FOUR

As they drove along Unter den Linden, Carter could see the Brandenburg Gate sharply outlined by the lights of the wall. He slowed and turned left into Friedrichstrasse. They were five hundred yards from Checkpoint Charlie.

Just short of Kronenstrasse, he parked.

It was 9:45.

"You take it from here."

"What?" Pavel cried. "Aren't you going over with me?"

"It's safer if you go over alone. Let me check your papers one more time."

Pavel handed over the passport and visa he had already gotten from Carter. Pretending to study it, Carter watched the nervous little man out of the corner of his eye.

He had given Pavel back his bottle. When he saw the man tip the bottle to his lips, Carter snaked his hand inside his jacket pocket and withdrew the Rudolph Press passport.

"Here."

Pavel pocketed it without a glance.

The Killmaster opened the heating vents wide, directing both toward the driver. Then he flipped a toggle switch just under the dash.

"Just hit the toggle," Marty Jacobs had said, "and get the hell out. You'll have twenty minutes."

Carter got out of the car as Pavel slid over.

"I don't like this," the little man whimpered.

"Just stay cool, Ilya," Carter said, patting him on the shoulder. "You'll be fine."

"I'm afraid."

"Of course you're afraid, but just keep in mind all the things Greta promised you in the West."

"Yes, yes, that's true."

Pavel's body trembled visibly and his face was bathed in sweat. Carter hoped he made it as far as the checkpoint.

Carter stood in the darkened doorway of a decayed apartment building. He was about forty yards from the wide-open, free-fire zone leading to Checkpoint Charlie. On either side of the road, the crisscross of tank traps indicated the limits of the mine fields.

It was 9:55.

Test number two had been pased. The girl, Bruna, had played out her part just as the Turk, Nomali, had said she would.

Harry Jens.

Anton Nomali.

Both clean.

That left only one.

Slowly Carter released the breath he had been holding.

He noticed that there was more activity at the gate now. A small truckload of armed Vopos had arrived. A big black Czechoslovakian Tatra—the Cadillac of the East—swerved around the truck. It rocked to a halt and two men emerged from the rear seat.

At this distance Carter couldn't be sure, but he thought he saw stars on their shoulder boards.

The setup was in high gear.

Then he saw Pavel. The little man was inching the Volkswagen into the narrow lane leading to the checkpoint. The yellow lights bathed the car.

Carter desperately wanted a cigarette, but now wasn't the time.

Suddenly, a spotlight came on, then another, and another. All of them rolled in a search pattern and stopped on the Volkswagen.

Pavel panicked, just as Carter thought he would. He threw the car into reverse, but it was too late. Vopo armored cars and light trucks swarmed in behind the Volkswagen, blocking it off.

The Killmaster started to glance at his watch. He didn't have to. There was an explosion of flame inside the car and a bone-chilling scream.

The car door burst open. Pavel, still screaming with his hands to his melted face, rolled out. He struggled to his feet and, clawing at his eyes, made a complete turn.

Evidently he could still see a little because he ran away from the lights, toward the darkness.

The firing came from all sides. Slugs tore into Pavel's body, literally lifting it from the ground.

Miraculously, he came back down on his feet. He staggered back toward the Volkswagen.

The firing continued, into Pavel and the car. It stopped only when Pavel's body slid motionless to the concrete.

Carter didn't wait for the rest of it. He turned and, keeping in the shadows of the buildings, walked back down Friedrichstrasse. As he crossed Alexanderplatz he lit a cigarette.

Ilya Pavel hadn't known. But then he wouldn't. It was far more effective if the Russian really thought he was heading West.

Carter climbed the stairs and rapped on the door.

"Who is it?"

"Your friendly Swiss from Zurich."

The door opened immediately. Bruna's face was a pasty white. "What happened?"

"I've got to use one of your chairs tonight," Carter said. "I'll be out early in the morning."

"My God, you didn't make it," she gasped.

"Oh, I made it."

At noon Carter walked to the Bahnhof Friedrichstrasse. He had to wait only five minutes for the overhead S-Bahn linking East and West.

A Vopo checked his Ames Johnson passport and his visa with the current day's stamp on it.

"You just came over at nine this morning, mein Herr. Your visa is good until midnight."

"I know," Carter replied, smiling, "but my girl friend had to work today."

"Oh . . ."

Thirty minutes later he got off at Bahnhof Zoo with a crush of people. A cab took him to the hotel.

He informed the desk that he would be checking out in an hour. From room service he ordered a large breakfast. He rummaged in the mini-bar until he found a miniature of Chivas, and headed for the shower.

By the time he was a new man and dressed, the breakfast had arrived.

He ate leisurely and then packed. He had left the automatic he'd gotten from the old man in the church with Bruna. She would know how to get rid of it. Now he took his Luger, the shoulder rig, and a silencer from the false compartment of his bag.

The weight felt good under his arm.

He didn't have to formally check out. The voucher he had signed would solve that problem. He carried his bag past the desk and into the street.

"Forty-eight Englestrasse," he told the taxi driver, "and I want you to wait for me."

Amalgamated Press and Wire Services of Berlin—cover for the AXE staff—was on the top floor of a twelve-story building.

Carter smiled at the pretty blond receptionist, went through a steel door into the inner sanctum.

He wove his way through desks and computers to Marty Jacobs's private office. The head of AXE Berlin gave a sigh of relief when he saw Carter.

"Thank God it wasn't you."

Carter shook his head and dropped into a chair. "Ilya Pavel."

"The device in the Volkswagen worked?"

"Like a charm," Carter said. "It should be a week before they decide it wasn't me." He tossed the manila folder onto the desk. "Here's what Pavel had to offer. It all looks routine, but the research people might find something good in it."

Jacobs leaned back, letting his eyelids fall to half-mast. "Is it finished?"

"No, but I'll dictate the report up to this point."

Jacobs nodded and punched a button on his desk. Carter had an N3, Killmaster, designation. Jacobs didn't. The written report would include only what had occurred on the mission up to this point. Whatever wet work Carter did from this point on would be verbally reported, face-to-face, with the chief of AXE at Dupont Circle in Washington, David Hawk.

"I need a couple of things done," Carter growled.

"Anything."

"Get me a ticket to Frankfurt. I think there's a five-ten flight. Have someone take my bag to the airport and check it."

"Sure. Tickets will be at the counter. Anything else?"

"Yeah." Carter tossed a piece of paper over the desk. "Call that number at two-thirty sharp this afternoon. Tell her you have news—you have to see her pronto."

"You got it," Jacobs replied. "How about connections on from Frankfurt?"

Carter smiled. "I'll handle them myself."

As he walked into the outer office, Carter was sure he could already hear the *bouzouki* music.

Carter took the inside rear stairs from the basement garage. He timed it so he reached her floor at exactly 2:30. Through the door he heard the telephone ring.

Her voice was muffled. Two minutes later he heard the locks click. The door flew open and she stepped into the hall struggling into her coat.

She was in Carter's arms before she ever knew he was there. "You . . . Nick?"

Carter put on his longest face. "Yeah. Let's talk."

She was good, damn good. She got her composure back before Carter got her back into the apartment and the door closed.

"How did it go?"

"You mean you haven't heard?"

"No, how could I? Marty Jacobs just called. He wanted me to meet him."

Bullshit, Carter thought, *so much bullshit. You knew*

fifteen minutes after Pavel fried that you had a stiff. Only problem is, you thought the stiff was me.

"How about a drink? I'll tell you all about it."

"Sure."

She tossed her coat on a nearby chair and glided behind a worn wicker bar. She wore white, figure-hugging slacks and a sweater that left nothing to the imagination. The color accentuated her drawn face, the rigidity that had crept into her athletic body since he had guided her through the door.

"What would you like?"

"Chivas, neat, if you've got it."

"Coming right up. What happened?"

"Pavel got it at Charlie."

Her face almost collapsed, but she managed to hold it. But her hand shook a little pouring the scotch. "How?"

"I saw it all," Carter said, "from a doorway. I'd say they put about a hundred slugs into him."

"Oh, my God." She put the drink on the bar and her hands disappeared.

Carter sipped from the glass with his left hand. "Yeah, it reminded me of Hauser a year ago."

She winced. She was a dynamic woman, good nerves, but her thoughts were mirrored in her face, her body. It was an attractive body, energetic, sensuous, and younger than her age.

For just a second Carter sensed her as a woman.

It passed and he spoke again.

"Of course Hauser was walking across when they nailed him. Not even an *'Achtung! Halt!'* They just cut him in half. Pavel almost had a fighting chance if he had kept his head. He was in a car."

Her head jerked up. "But you—"

"Yeah, I know, Greta. I was supposed to go over in

the Volks at ten. Pavel was walking over at midnight. I changed my mind."

"Lucky for you that you did."

"Yeah." Carter finished his drink.

"A year's work," she sighed, taking her drink and moving around the bar toward the desk, "gone."

"Couldn't have been much work. I had a conversation with Pavel. He'd been looking under every rock for a year trying to find someone he could defect to and help him get out."

She managed a laugh. "And along I came."

"I don't think so, Greta. I think you were there all the time. What were you going to do with Pavel? Were you going to let Jens and Nomali pick him up and take him in? Or did you have a shooter somewhere to take him out when he came across?"

With incredible speed her hand dived into a drawer and came up with a Beretta .380. She raised her arm and Carter heard the click as she cocked it.

Then she paused, eyes wide. Wilhelmina, the Luger, an ugly silencer attached, was pointed at the sweater's indentation between her large breasts.

"Stalemate," Carter growled.

"I'm an expert shot," she hissed.

"So am I."

"Then we kill each other."

He shrugged. "If that's the way you want it."

It seemed like hours. It was less than a minute.

"We're acting like idiots," she said quietly.

Carter said nothing.

She uncocked the Beretta and gently laid it on the desk. Carter picked it up and slid it into his jacket pocket. Then he holstered the Luger.

"How long, Greta?"

She shrugged. "I've been a sleeper with the BfV for fifteen years. They activated me three years ago."

"When you started working with us?"

She nodded. "Shall we go? The second they hear I am blown, they will start negotiations to bring me back."

"Yeah, I know."

Her instinct for self-preservation must have warned her. Carter had his hand on her arm. As he started to slide it up to her throat, she made a claw of her right hand and went for his eyes.

Carter blocked it, but she got her shoulder into his chest. She was a big woman, strong.

They hit the carpet together and rolled, one over the other. The lust for survival gave her some bit of equality.

Then she was immobilized beneath Carter's weight. She glared at him with an expression of murderous hatred.

With an animal scream she rolled over on her stomach, but she couldn't dislodge him. He waited until she had raised herself on her hands and knees, then he leaped onto her back. With his feet pressed against the wall behind him, he thrust his right knee between her thighs and ground her into the carpet.

He moved his hands up until his thumbs found the pressure points.

She knew, and tried harder to buck him from her body.

But it was too late.

Already the blood was being cut off from her brain. Not too much. Not enough to kill her, just enough to knock her out for an hour or so.

She went limp beneath him.

Carter caught his breath. He washed both glasses and

replaced them behind the bar. He hung up her coat and then carried her into the kitchen.

The window was tightly sealed. There was only one door. Carter carefully rolled two heavy bath towels and placed them near the bottom of the door. He unwound a pair of coat hangers and hooked their ends around the rolled towels.

He sat Greta Hommler at the table, her head on her folded arms. There was a gas heater in the wall and a four-burner stove with an oven. He extinguished the pilot lights of both.

After taking a last check for any other way the gas might escape, he turned the oven and all four burners on, as well as the heater.

One last rubdown of the apartment removed any possible fingerprints.

Carefully, he closed the door, running the hangers underneath. Then he tugged the towels into place to seal the crack. This done, he turned the hangers sideways and withdrew them from beneath the towels.

Downstairs, he walked to the nearest U-Bahn station and took a train to the Tiergarten. There, he took the blue express train to the airport.

The flight was five minutes late but made up the time in the air. In Frankfurt, he claimed his bag and sent a cable to Amalgamated Press and Wire Services, G. Bateman, Dupont Circle, Washington, D.C., USA:

AM ON TO VERY IMPORTANT STORY IN-
VOLVING EFFECTS OF MEDITERRANEAN
SUN AND CHIVAS REGAL ON TANNING
PROCESS STOP EXPECT RESEARCH TAKE 2
PERHAPS 3 WEEKS STOP BERLIN PROB-
LEM TERMINATED STOP
CARTER

At the Olympic Airlines counter, he presented his passport and credit card.

"Yes, Mr. Carter?"

"One way to Athens, please."

FIVE

The skipper's name was Damos, just Damos. He was a monster of a man with a face the color of burned leather. His eyes were pale for a Greek, and his nose was arrogant. A mane of white hair blew in the wind as he guided the cruiser through the soft swells.

Carter stood beside him at the helm.

"There she is, two points to port."

Carter squinted along the Greek's upraised arm. The *Noble Savage* was about a mile away, riding easily at anchor.

She was a solitary beauty against the setting sun and the blue water. Converted into a floating pleasure palace ten years before by Chandra Braxton, the yacht had started out on the Tyne in England as a minesweeper.

It was painted a dazzling white. Even from a distance Carter could see every line of its huge, elegant hull. Its brasswork glittered and its ropework was pipe-clayed to the snowy virginity of a fleecy cloud.

On board was a helicopter, a swimming pool, two powerboats, a three-piece band, and a Cordon Bleu chef.

Its crew and officers were Greek except for a Scottish skipper. Most of them had left a cruise line because Chandra Braxton paid them more money and the work was more more exciting. Carter knew that, to a man, they were loyal to her to the death.

Carter had stopped in Athens just long enough to pick up a bathing suit, some shirts and sun shorts, evening wear, and to make a shore-to-ship telephone call.

"Nick, how lovely! Where are you?"

"Athens. I just got in an hour or so ago."

"I could send the helicopter, but it's down for a few hours."

"No problem, I'll get a charter. Where are you?"

"About four miles off Mykonos. Ask for Captain Damos. He'll ferry you out. How long have you?"

"As long as you'll put up with me."

She had laughed, long and loud. "Don't say that—you'll never see the States again." Her voice lowered to a serious tone. "How did it go?"

"Well."

"Good. I'm having a small party tonight, about twenty guests. I drop them off in the morning and then there's just you and me."

It was Carter's turn to laugh. "And fifty staff and crew."

"Ah, but they're discreet."

Captain Damos laid back on the throttles and his two sons rolled the rubber fenders over the side. The *Noble Savage* loomed at their side.

"Beautiful, eh?" Damos said.

Carter nodded. "Beautiful indeed—a place fit for royalty."

Damos laughed. "The lady probably has more money than most kings."

Up close, the swift elegance of the yacht's fighting ship lines were more pronounced.

The cruiser eased up to the lader steps and Carter hopped off. One of Damos's boys was already up the ladder with Carter's bags. When he was back on board, Damos waved and swerved the cruiser around the *Savage*'s prow, toward Mykonos.

A white-uniformed steward waited at the top of the ladder. "Mr. Carter?"

Carter nodded and the steward exploded into a salute. He picked up the two bags. "Madame Braxton will join you shortly. A matter of business. She'll be conferring with her secretary and lawyers for about an hour. Your cabin is this way."

Carter followed him aft toward an awning-covered fantail, and then into the passenger cabin area. They moved forward on the mezzanine deck. He had already guessed where his cabin would be . . . right next to Chandra's master suite, with an unlocked connecting door.

He was right.

"The bar is here, sir, the bath there. You can call for anything you need with this console by the bed."

"I know," Carter said, "thank you."

"Yes, sir." The steward gave him a slight bow and backed out of the cabin with a tight grin on his lips.

The furnishings were shipboard but the best money could buy. Teak dominated the bedroom, and the bath was all Italian marble. A Canaletto hung above the small bar. Carter knew that there were a few more Canalettos, a couple of Picassos, and a Renoir scattered around the ship.

"My only aesthetic vice," Chandra often said.

Carter built a scotch and unpacked. He was heading

for the bar a second time when he heard a light rap on the connecting door.

"Come in."

She did, in a pair of black silk lounging pajamas and rhinestone-encrusted sandals.

"Jesus, am I glad to see you," she enthused. "I even left my lawyers hanging. It must be love."

"You look like Bloomingdale's."

"I know . . . to match my boring guests."

She glided into his arms smelling fresh and expensive. He kissed her and ran his hands under her pajama top. She wasn't wearing a bra.

"Mmm, good," she sighed into his ear, "you missed me."

"Want a drink?"

She nodded. "Glass of wine."

He poured. When he turned back, she was on the bed, naked. "That's what I like about you, right to the heart of the matter," he chuckled.

She took the glass. "Money makes us all avaricious. But I'm only trampish in a dilettante, friends-only way." She patted the bed beside her.

Carter kicked his shoes off and lay down. "What's on for the evening?"

"Drinks at seven, dinner at nine. It's partly social, partly business."

"Anyone I know?"

She laughed. "Oh, yes, several, if only by reputation. Remember the business I'm in."

"Getting ready to start a little war somewhere?"

"Don't preach, Nick darling. What they do with my toys is their business. If I didn't provide, someone else would."

There was a hard edge to her voice that Carter recognized. The fact that her former husband had made his millions in arms, and Chandra had expanded the empire into a billion or so, was always a ticklish point between them.

"Not to worry," he said. "If everybody loved everybody, I'd be out of a job."

She traced a line down his face with a finger and went to work unbuttoning his shirt. "Do you know Joanna Lloyd?"

"Can't say as I do." He let his hand trail along the smooth line of her hip.

"Married to Senator Samuel Lloyd."

"Met him once," Carter said. "Do-gooder, dove with pure white feathers. Wants to reform the world."

Chandra laughed and went for his belt. "That's Sam. I tried to seduce him once, shocked the hell out of him. Sam's an old friend. I don't know Joanna very well."

"So?" Carter said, swallowing the last of his drink and losing the glass.

"Sam and Joanna are having a problem or two. He called me, wanted me to watch over her for a couple of weeks."

"So it won't be just us and the crew?"

"She got here this morning. Sam sounded a little desperate. I couldn't say no."

Carter remembered Samuel Lloyd. "Well, she can knit on the fantail while we party."

Chandra's eyes twinkled. "I don't think this one goes for knitting."

"What does that mean?"

"You'll see when you meet her."

Carter didn't have a chance to speak again. He was naked and Chandra was going to work.

She was beautiful in the nude, the soft hair falling around her face in gentle waves. He was aroused. He leaned forward and kissed her tenderly. At the same time, he lifted his hand and cupped her breast.

Bells rang. Her breasts were large and firm. He put his arms around her and drove his tongue into her warm mouth.

Her pelvis began a slow circular movement against him. It felt as if molten lead had been poured into his veins.

He stroked her thighs, then cupped his hand over her mound with a deliberately abrupt and possessive touch.

She was warm and open.

His tension was so strong that he felt he would explode. Her slender fingers moved around him, heightening his desire still more. Her body swayed beneath his hand with the regularity of a pendulum.

"Enough," she sighed.

"Not nearly enough," he growled.

"I mean, of that."

Spreading her legs and lifting her knees, she tugged him up over her body. She circled her arms around his neck and thrust her hips forward with a groan.

Carter took her with a single thrust that made their pubic bones collide. In seconds they were both panting and their movements had matched each other's rhythms. It was wild and wonderful and Carter told her so.

Then she bent her legs, as though to bring him even more deeply into her. Despite her uncomfortable position she moaned ecstatically, with her lips pressed against his neck. This sophisticated, elegant woman seemed to get incredible pleasure from being taken roughly.

He put his hands behind her and pushed against her even harder. He felt pleasure sliding down his spine and into his belly, violent and irresistible, as if it were the first time he had ever made love. He exploded, sooner than he would have liked. She tried to open her legs still wider, in an uncontrollable spasm. Her fingernails sank into his neck. He heard her cry out.

They stayed still for a few seconds with the blood pounding in their temples, oblivious of everything around them. Then she began moving her shapely hips again, impaled and happy. She looked up at him.

"Something else I have to tell you."

"What's that?"

"Just remember, Joanna Lloyd is married."

He didn't get a chance to comment. Her hips were already moving again and he felt new life between his legs.

Happy hour was in full swing by the time Carter hit the forward deck and the pool area. The small band had set up forward near a part of the deck cleared for dancing. There were two bars, port and starboard of the pool. The band played Muzak just under the guests' chatter, and stewards scooted everywhere with an endless supply of drinks.

Carter eased around the perimeter to the starboard bar and ordered a Chivas. It came and he sipped as he started to survey the guests. A few he recognized. There was the Count of Something and the Baron of Something Else. He spotted a Roman starlet and a Hollywood starlet from their pictures in newspapers. The rest were a wide assortment liberally sprinkled with business types.

He guessed a high percentage of them were Chandra's Swiss and English bankers. There must be a good-sized deal afoot.

"Hello."

He turned. She was tall, in flouncy black. Her hair was tinted a pinkish blond, and her face was deeply

tanned, the rich, exclusive kind of tan that one only
acquires in the south of France and eventually seams the
face.

"Hello."

"Dora Gimbel." She extended a hand and Carter
shook it.

"Nick Carter."

"Good. I like a man who shakes a woman's hand
instead of slobbering over it."

She seemed to lean forward a little further with each
word. The front of her gown was extremely low-cut and
she word no bra. In the light Carter could see clear
down into the deep valley between her breasts and trace
the line of flesh clear to her dark areolas.

She saw him looking and smiled. "You don't fit."

"What?" he asked.

"This horde. Unless you belong to Chandra . . ."

Before Carter could reply, a tall, gray-haired man in
a white sharkskin dinner jacket, black trousers, and a
cherry-colored cummerbund stepped partially between
them.

"Dora, must you?" he hissed out of the side of his
mouth.

"Must I what, darling?"

"Hang your breasts out to every man on the ship."

"Why, Monte, I'm surprised you even noticed I still
had them." She turned to Carter. "This is my husband,
Monte. He's quite boring but very rich."

"Nick Carter." Monte Gimbel's hand was soft and
damp.

"How do you do?" Gimbel said. "Please don't think
too ill of my mate. She fancies herself a *femme fatale*.
Quite ridiculous at her age, of course. Notice the sunken
cheeks and the huge hips?"

"Screw you, Monte," Dora said.

Carter could see a marital war brewing. He was looking for a way to extricate himself, when Chandra did it for him.

"Monte, Dora, I see you've met Nick," she purred, grasping Carter's arm and steering him in another direction. "Please excuse us, I must introduce him to the other guests."

Carter let her tug him along. "Thanks."

"I know," she muttered. "They're really not destructive, except to each other."

"Nice dress, if that's what it is."

Chandra laughed. "I think it's clever."

She was dressed in what appeared to be no more than a collection of scarves, layer over layer. Gold and silver wrapped turban style around her hair. A paisley print flowed in a nice line over her breasts and middle. African prints wound low on her hips to form a skirt that fell to her ankle on one side and barely to the middle of the thigh on the other. The finishing touches were a wide leather belt and a collection of chain belts draped across her hips.

Her only jewelry was a pair of emerald earrings that matched her eyes and dangled to her collarbones.

As they worked their way through the guests, Carter tried to register the names for the first few minutes and then gave up.

"Oh, there's Joanna," Chandra said. "Come along."

Joanna Lloyd was quite beautiful in a rather hard way. Her figure, in a long silver sheath dress slit up the front, was somewhere between voluptuous and overblown. It was the kind of figure that stayed merely voluptuous as long as its owner stayed on Ry-Krisp and lettuce.

A great braid of golden hair was wrapped around her head and her eyes were a deep, intense blue. Her face had regular features . . . broad, but not heavy, with typical Slavic cheek structure. Carter judged that she was in her late twenties.

"Joanna," Chandra said, "I want you to meet my good friend Nick Carter."

She held out her hand to him at once. The palm was cool, slightly moist, the bones delicate but not fragile. There was a toughness about her for all her beauty.

"I'm very pleased to meet you, Mr. Carter." Her voice was soft, low-pitched, the accent almost English.

"My pleasure," Carter said.

"Nick is with the State Department."

The change in Joanna Lloyd's face was instant. Carter was smiling, but no smile came back. She gave him a stiff, barely perceptible nod, and the way she looked at him was both startling and disconcerting. He sensed that there was no friendliness here. The long-lashed eyes suddenly seemed openly resentful and tinged with what could have been contempt.

"If you'll excuse me," she said, and scurried away.

Carter turned to Chandra. "Something I said?"

Chandra looked perplexed. "I don't know. Maybe it was something *I* said."

Carter didn't reply. Over her shoulder, he saw a cruiser pulling up to the side of the *Noble Savage*. Seconds later, Zax Feeyad appeared at the rail.

"Chandra," Carter said, steel in his voice, "what the hell is that bastard doing here?"

"Zax? Why, Nick, he's the guest of honor."

SIX

Zax Feeyad was a squat barrel of a man with an immense breadth of shoulder that even so seemed only just wide enough to sustain the weight of his head. The head was vast, with a great weight of white hair, a nose like a ship's prow, a rich, sensitive mouth, and wide gray eyes that had never told anybody anything. The whole effect was of a crude but tremendous power. He had the force, the will, and the strength to achieve almost anything he wanted. And he'd done so.

No one really knew where Feeyad was from, where he was born. The story went that he had first sprouted in the Algerian war of independence, selling information to the French side and guns to the rebel side.

He came out of that war rich, and went onto others, mostly in Africa—Rhodesia, Angola, Swaziland. He quickly multiplied the first million he had made in Algeria ten times over. Legitimately, he bought real estate all over the world as well as shipping and, lately, mining shares. Illegally, he bought and manipulated governments, started wars for his own profit, and had anyone who got in his way terminated.

The last file Carter had seen on Zax Feeyad had the man buying his way into South African citizenship.

Chandra hadn't answered his question about what the hell Feeyad was doing aboard the *Noble Savage*. The steward had announced dinner.

Now, Feeyad sat between Chandra and Joanna Lloyd at the opposite end of the table. Carter had drawn the Count of Something and Dora Gimbel as his dining partners.

Throughout the meal, the big man kept glancing Carter's way, as if he knew him but couldn't place him. It was unlikely. AXE people had been assigned to turn over rocks in Feeyad's past and present, but Carter had never been one of them. Of course nothing concretely incriminating had ever been unearthed. Feeyad was always several layers away from the actual dirty work.

The Count of Something was rating the finest resorts in the world, from the Mamounia in Morocco to Hotel du Cap on the Riviera. Carter tried his best to pay attention while fighting off Dora Gimbel whose hand kept crawling up the inside of his thigh.

He breathed a sigh of relief when the meal was over and he could escape to the bar. He was on his second brandy when Joanna Lloyd moved in beside him.

"Hello." She was smiling now, her eyes playing coy little games that didn't suit her.

"Hello."

"I would like to apologize. I was rude."

Carter shrugged. "How's the senator?"

"You know my husband?"

"We've met."

"I thought you were a watchdog."

"What?"

"I thought my husband sent you to watch me."

"Why would he do that?"

"Because I have this little vice. I sleep around. Chandra says you're a marvelous dancer. Would you like to dance?"

Carter led her to the front of the pool and she glided into his arms. For her size and the top-heavy quality of her figure, she moved gracefully, anticipating his every touch.

"You do dance well," she said with a smile.

"So do you."

She giggled. It didn't fit. "I used to dance professionally. What do you do for the State Department?"

"Push papers, sign papers. Sometimes I'm a messenger boy."

Another dancer lurched toward them. Carter evaded the collision by lifting her easily and swinging her around.

"You're very strong," Joanna said, "for a messenger boy."

"I used to work out," Carter replied, deadpan.

"Are you stationed in Washington?"

"Most of the time. I'm on vacation."

What the hell is this, Carter thought, *a third degree*?

"How did you meet Chandra? Isn't she lovely?"

"Lovely." Carter tugged her to him. She lifted her arms, moved to his touch, and ground her pelvis against his. "I think Chandra used to sleep with my husband."

"Probably business," Carter said gruffly. "How often do you sleep around?"

"Often. Are you interested?"

"I'll let you know."

"I'm looking forward to sailing around the Med for a couple of weeks, just the three of us."

"It should be interesting," Carter said.

She giggled again. "C'mon, I'll show you just *how* interesting!"

She tugged him toward the stern of the ship. Carter was reluctant, but he followed her down the ladder to the fantail and the helicopter pad. She drew him into a pool of shadow behind it.

"Now nobody can see us," she cooed, wiggling her shoulders. Her dress peeled off her shoulders and gathered at her waist, leaving her breasts bare. "Now let's dance some more."

Her arms came around him again, and her mouth found his. She kissed him with a demanding skill that immediately set his body on fire. Her hands loosened the button of his jacket and slipped inside it, roaming delicately over his ribs, across his back. Carter wondered if he was being searched, in the most tactful way possible, to see if he carried a gun.

Warning bells started going off in his head. First the third degree and now this. It was all a little too fast and a little too blatant, even if the lovely Mrs. Lloyd was and outright nymphomaniac.

"I love to dance like this," she moaned.

Her hands caught his and brought them to her bare breasts. Carter reacted normally to her soft flesh for just a moment and then caught her wrists.

"I just remembered someone I've got to see."

"Later."

"Now." He headed toward the ladder.

"Come back here!" she hissed.

He left her tugging back into her dress and hit the forward hatch leading down to the main companionway. It was locked.

He ran around the deck and took the steps down three at a time. He almost butted chests with Zax Feeyad coming up.

"Ah, Mr. Carter, I don't think we've met. Zax Feeyad."

Carter shook the proffered hand. The grip was like steel. Feeyad's cold eyes checked him like a side of beef. Dead beef.

"Chandra has been telling me about you."

"Oh?"

"Yes, everyone in Washington interests me. I must be leaving. It's a pity. I would enjoy talking with you. Perhaps we shall meet again."

Carter nodded. "Yes, perhaps we will."

Feeyad hefted his bulk on up the ladder and disappeared. Carter went on down the companionway to his cabin. It wasn't locked. There couldn't possibly be thieves on board the *Noble Savage*.

He checked the room. Nothing seemed to be out of place, but then he hadn't taken the precautions he would normally take in the field. After all he was on vacation, why should he?

The drawers were undisturbed and his clothes seemed to be hanging with the same space between each garment in the closet.

Then his eye fell on his bag.

He pulled it out and tossed it on the bed. In the bottom he used his fingernail under the leather and peeled back just a fraction of it. Then he hit the three hidden catch releases with his thumb. Before peeling the leather all the way back, he checked the two normal locks in the bag's handle.

A fine strip of red shown in both of them.

Someone had just had a look inside the secret compartment of his bag.

The party broke up about three in the morning. Carter hadn't wanted any more of it. He undressed and slumped across the bed in his cabin with a scotch and the television.

He must have dozed off. The noise of a door closing in Chandra's adjoining master cabin awakened him. He slipped from the bed, pulled on a robe, and moved to the door.

Chandra was standing at the foot of the bed. The scarf dress was just hitting the floor. She turned and posed in her beige lingerie.

"I wondered what happened to you."

There was a robe lying across the foot of the bed. Carter tossed it to her and, carrying his own glass, moved to the bar.

"Let's talk."

"My, my, we're in a mood."

"What's your story with Zax Feeyad?"

"Nick, let's get something straight. I don't ask you your business, you don't ask mine."

"All right, later for that." He dropped into a chair. "What's the scoop on Joanna Lloyd?"

"What do you mean, 'scoop'?"

"I think you know what I mean, Chandra."

"Oh, dear. What happened?" He hadn't offered to fix her a drink. She moved to the bar and fixed her own.

Carter told her about their dancing, what Joanna had said, and then the mini-seduction on the fantail. For the moment he stopped short of telling her about his suspicions.

Chandra sighed and folded her body into the lounger across from him. She pulled her knees up under her chin, letting the robe fall open.

Carter paid no attention.

"I don't know her very well. As a matter of fact I only met her once, about a month ago, in Washington, at a party."

"She's pretty open about her sleeping habits," Carter said dryly. "Is it true?"

"Must be," Chandra said, and shrugged. "Sam told me he came home a few nights ago and found her with some young kid . . . in bed. From his tone I gathered it wasn't the first time."

"Why does he put up with it?"

She chuckled low in her throat. "Something you and I wouldn't understand, Nick. He's in love with her."

"So he sends her off to you? Come on, Chandra, you're no baby-sitter. You don't do shit for nothing. What's up?"

Chandra studied her drink and then him. "Sam is extremely busy right now, something very important with the United Nations. He can't spend much time with her and, evidently, little Joanna is a woman who needs time."

"Okay," Carter said, "what's in it for you?"

One eyebrow arched sharply. "Do you really think I'm so mercenary?"

"Yes," Carter said, nodding, "I do."

She studied him for another moment and then stood. "All right." She started to pace.

The robe was slinky. It followed every movement of her body. Carter kept his mind on his drink and the subject matter.

"I owe Sam a couple of favors."

"What kind of favors?"

"Inside information. I have some pretty heavy natural gas, oil, and mine stocks in Namibia. Sam is lobbying pretty hard in the U.N. to get a ruling to have everyone kicked out of Namibia and declaring the country an independent republic."

"What would happen to your stocks if that happened?"

She paused in front of him. "Chances are they would be worthless."

"So you're trying to get Senator Sam to change his tune." Suddenly Carter had a vile taste in his mouth.

"No, not at all," Chandra replied, sliding onto his lap. "I just want the real skinny on the vote *before* it becomes public."

"So you can dump your stocks?"

She nodded. "You can't blame me for that."

"No," he sighed, "I guess I can't. What's Sam's position?"

"He contends it's better for Namibia to be independent, even if it goes socialist. Right now, the countries that have a big piece of controlling Namibia are essentially raping her. If it keeps up, Sam contends there will be a rebellion and the Communists will take power. Then we all lose anyway."

Carter thought about this as her fingers went to work on the back of his neck. The top of her robe opened. Her breasts bulged lustily above the cups of her bra.

"Nick . . ."

"Yeah?"

Her lips found his, warmly and passionately. He couldn't stop his arms from curling around her and drawing her close. Then her lips brushed across his ear. "Have you forgotten you're on holiday?"

He opened the robe further and kissed her where the cleavage of her breasts rose above the lace of her lingerie. She pressed his head against her breast and kissed him on his upturned cheek.

"It would be better in bed, darling," she whispered.

They lay together between the cool sheets, her body against his, her head resting on his chest. He could feel a trickle of perspiration from her forehead. His hand gently stroked back her thick hair, feeling its faint dampness, stirring its clean scent.

"You're thinking again," she said.

"I know."

"Must you?"

Without warning she wormed one leg under his body and rolled him between her thighs.

"What are you thinking now?" she chuckled.

"How I'm going to be able to stand two weeks of this."

He could sense it was morning. He opened his eyes. Sunlight and a fresh breeze came through the porthole that opened over the lower deck.

Chandra was sitting on a bench before a dressing table, slowly brushing her hair. He watched the rhythmic movement of the brush and the slow sweep of her hair against the soft cream of her neck. She sat erect, her head thrown back, her back straight, curving gently into the firm buttocks that rested on the velvet cushion. She was beautiful. He gave an involuntary sigh and she turned around with a dazzling smile.

"Good morning."

He didn't speak but rose and walked over to her, bending to embrace her, his palms cupping her firm breasts. He kissed her behind the left ear and she straightened with a faint tremble as her left hand rose to stroke the side of his head.

"Breakfast here?"

"Yes. I'm not interested in the world at the moment."

"Croissants, café au lait, orange juice?"

"Sounds terrific," he said.

They ate on the little balcony. The morning sun flooded the white damask cloth, the cheerful rose motif of the breakfast service, and the warm brown rolls. A small bouquet of three jonquils in a crystal bud vase blended with the pale yellow of butter flakes on ice and the deep orange of the freshly squeezed juice.

As she poured his coffee, Carter suddenly laughed. "You know something? I've never seen you pour a cup of coffee."

"It's like riding a bicycle and fucking, darling," Chandra said between clenched teeth, "you never forget how."

Carter held up his hands, palms out. "Truce. I'll be nice for two weeks, I promise." He bit into a croissant. "Your guests get off?"

She nodded. "All except for Joanna, of course."

"You didn't see them off?"

"I said good-bye last night."

He dropped it. When one had as much money as Chandra Braxton, one didn't see people to the door.

"Joanna would like to sail over to Piraeus for a day of sightseeing. Any objections?"

"None," he said.

"Good. I have one last bit of work this morning. From this afternoon I'm free."

She brushed his cheek with her lips and headed for the bath. Carter went to his own cabin and pulled on a pair of trunks. He headed for the foredeck and the pool.

Joanna lay at the other end of the pool on an air mattress, her body glistening with oil.

Carter waved and she turned away.

Be nice, he told himself, *be nice*.

He went into the pool and did ten laps in a slow, easy crawl. Then he rolled to his back and backstroked ten more, coming up just beside where Joanna lay.

"Good morning."

She just nodded. He couldn't see her eyes behind the dark glasses.

He climbed out of the pool and a steward handed him a towel.

"A drink, sir?"

"What's the lady having?"

"Orange juice and champagne," the man replied.

"I'll share hers," Carter said.

He dried himself and checked out Joanna from the corner of his eye. He saw a blue bikini top filled to overflowing, and above it a very stern, tight-lipped face topped with a towel around her blond hair. The bottom half of the bikini was equally well filled, and everything bare was well tanned.

"You have a nice tan."

"Thank you."

"You're quite beautiful, really, especially when you smile."

She didn't smile, but she raised her glasses. "Who are you?"

He shrugged and stretched out on the next chaise. "Just a gigolo, a hanger-on. Free drinks, free airplane and boat rides. You know."

"Bullshit," she said, and dropped her glasses back over her eyes.

Carter filled her glass and another for himself.

She was in profile now and looked even younger. Her nose had a cute tilt, and above it the lashes were thick and long. She was, he admitted, a very attractive kid when viewed objectively. And perhaps that was what bothered him the most. Well, the hell with her. She could be snooty, so could he.

"Who taught you your manners?" he said flatly.

For a moment he thought she was going to ignore him, and then, quite deliberately, she moved the glasses, slipped them on her nose, and looked at him as she might have with a lorgnette.

"I beg your pardon?"

"I was talking about manners. I wondered where you got your. You see, I was brought up to make a guest in the house feel welcome whether you particularly liked him or not. The idea was to be not just polite but gracious, to see to it that he felt at home while he was in your house."

"It's not my house," she said.

"Same thing. We're both Chandra's guests."

Suddenly she smiled and Carter got that cold feeling again, the one he had gotten when he had first met her the previous evening. "If I remember right, I tried to make you feel at home on the fantail last night."

"You call screwing a guest making him feel at home?"

"It's kicks. You want to be friendly, let's screw now."

"Lady, you're kinky," Carter said with a sigh, and lay back on the chaise.

"How much is my husband paying you to watch me?"

She was sitting up beside him, her weight supported on her arms that were thrust out behind her. The pose brought her torso into superb relief, emphasizing its rich curves, the firm, heavy roundness of flesh that the blue bikini did an irreducible minimum to conceal. Her eyes held his, then she breathed in, hard.

"You're going to lose your top," he said.

She breathed out in a burst of laughter, then leaned over him, the weight of her breasts just touching his chest, her lips soft on his mouth. His arms came around her, held her for a moment, then let her go.

"I'm sorry about last night. Honestly. I don't know what got into me. Truce?"

"Sure."

Her finger traced the deep scars across his shoulders

and chest. "You must have had a pretty bad accident . . . more than one."

"Skin diving," he said. "I cut myself on a clam shell. How long have you known Zax Feeyad?"

"Feeyad?" she sputtered. "I-I don't know him at all."

"I think you do."

She was a lousy actress. Only Chandra's arrival saved her.

"How about a swim, you two?"

"Sure," Carter said, and stood.

Joanna didn't move.

He and Chandra moved to the edge of the pool. She undid the cord of her robe and let it slip from her shoulders. Below it she wore a one-piece white swimsuit, cut high in the front, low in the back. Against it her skin was pale gold.

They hit the water as one and came up with their heads close together.

"Are you pissing her off," Chandra murmured in his ear, "or are you getting along with her?"

"Swimmingly," Carter said, "just swimmingly."

SEVEN

The sun was high in the sky but there was a cool breeze on the water. Across the water, which was far more brightly colored than Carter had ever thought water could be, the islands were clearly visible. Some were high, volcanic peaks with the clouds hanging over their summits; some were lying low in the water and fringed with trees; some were no more than piles of stone, their straggling trees fingering the sand at the water's edge. And some were hidden, dangerous reefs, concealing their sharp and treacherous faces under the water, waiting for the next subterranean swell to thrust them up into the sunlight, to become islands like the others.

The harbor they chose was a wide gash in the landscape well north of Pireaus. It was big enough for half a dozen boats to take complete shelter. Above, in honey-gold light, a few whitewashed houses clung to the rocky hillside that gave way to a green swath of olive trees, and then to a flattened rocky peninsula tipped by fir trees.

As they neared the coastline the sea seemed to

change from sapphire to turquoise, and then to aquamarine, as if someone had emptied all those jewels into the water.

They disembarked about fifteen minutes later onto a narrow harbor wall. There was a cluster of cottages there with sloping, red-tiled roofs, and one small taverna with a couple of fishermen sitting outside watching the *Noble Savage* ease its way to a mooring.

Chandra had called ahead and a snappy BMW convertible was waiting for them. Carter drove with Chandra beside him and Joanna in the back seat.

Dinner the night before had been dull and tense. Joanna seemed nervous all through the meal. And Chandra had sighed with relief when the other woman excused herself early.

Around eight, Senator Sam had called—not his wife, but Chandra—to find out how things were going.

"What did you tell him?" Carter had asked when she returned.

"That she's being a good girl."

"That should make him happy."

"Yes."

"What did he tell you?"

"That he's winning. One more vote should do it."

"Then you'll unload your stock?"

"I already did," she had said, smiling, "this morning."

Carter had quickly put two and two together. "To Zax Feeyad."

"That's right," she replied, obviously very pleased with herself.

"That's interesting, Chandra."

"Oh?"

"Yeah. I know Feeyad screws up countries, has people killed, is a man totally without morals or ethics. But it's my understanding that he's a good businessman."

"He is," she had shot back. "He's a damn good businessman."

"Then why, Chandra, did he buy worthless stocks?"

Her grin spread clear across her beautiful face. "He doesn't kow they are worthless, remember? It's little me, Chandra Braxton, who has the inside line with Senator Sam."

Carter wondered about that, but he had pursued it no further.

That morning the three of them had breakfast together. Joanna had been giggly and perky.

"I've got it all laid out, the route we'll take. It's up the coast road, here. We take the highway north to Dhafni, then the E90 to Thebes. But before we reach Thebes there's a little road into the mountains, here, where there is a delightful taverna . . ."

On and on she went. Carter and Chandra had just nodded.

Why not? they thought. Anything to keep the mercurial woman happy and amused.

Then, on the sail from the islands in, she had lapsed back into her surly, moody self, not speaking when spoken to, and obviously tense and nervous.

Now, as they put the top down on the car and prepared to leave, Joanna had to have something to drink. It couldn't wait. It had to be now.

"I'll get a large bottle of mineral water to take with us," she cried, and ran toward the taverna they had spotted coming in.

Carter and Chandra shook their heads and struggled to snap the trunk over the lowered top.

"Know what?" Carter murmured.

"Don't say it."

He did anyway. "For baby-sitting that one, Senator Sam owes you at least three freebies."

At last Joanna returned and they had set off.

Now they left the wide highway and headed due north through rolling hills.

They eased along for about four miles, with Joanna's face over the back of the front seat between them.

"There, right there to the right. That's the road to the taverna, Escos. We can stop there for lunch."

Carter slowed and made the turn. The road was dusty. During the rainy season it probably turned to mud. Once, long ago, an attempt had been made to gravel its surface. Only remnants remained and that had sifted to the sides, leaving a trench with potholes in the center.

The road also wound like a snake, both vertically and horizontally, with a few level straightaways now and then. It was on one of these that Carter noticed the dark Citroën SM. It made no attempt to close the distance between them and pass, even though Carter was crawling.

For God's sake, he told himself, *you're on vacation! Stop finding something sinister behind every bush!* The Citroën, he guessed, was hanging back to avoid their cloud of dust.

The road was hedged by eucalyptus trees and endless olive groves, their gnarled trunks taking strange shapes in the heat haze. Carter slowed for a small village. They could smell food aromas and see women scrubbing clothes in a small stream.

Beyond the village, the car dipped into a small valley and then began a steep climb between craggy rocks, grinding gravel under its wheels.

Carter's hands gripped the wheel hard as he wrestled the BMW around a tight curve at the crest of the grade.

A brief moment later he found himself slamming hard on the brake pedal, skidding the small car to a sliding stop.

"Wouldn't you know it," Chandra said. "They've got a flat."

They were staring at an obstacle in the narrow road. It was an old truck parked across their path, its fenders dented and rust flaking off its battered sides. Beside it, standing or leaning against the vehicle, three men watched dust rise around the BMW and disperse in the cool air. One of the men worked a jack, the other two watched.

Carter glanced in the rearview mirror. The Citroën was coming fast now. The three men in front started toward the Citroën.

"Shit," Carter hissed, and floored the BMW. At the same time, he spun the wheel. The convertible came around nicely and they too were heading for the Citroën.

"Nick, what is it?" Chandra cried.

"Who knows," he yelled over the screaming engine. "Bandits, maybe."

Fifty yards apart, the Citroën slewed sideways, completely blocking the road. Behind him, Carter could see all three of the men from the truck running up on the BMW. Two more poured out of the Citroën.

All five of them carried large-caliber Smith & Wesson revolvers.

Carter had no choice. He tromped the brakes and brought the BMW to a rocking halt.

The five men stopped a few paces from the car. All of them wore wide-brimmed straw hats and dark glasses, oversize and curved, concealing half their faces. Each of them also sported thick, jet-black mustaches.

The one on the right in front, a head taller than the others, spoke. "Throw your gun out!"

"I'm not armed," Carter yelled.

"Bullshit. Throw it out!"

So much for being on vacation, Carter thought. He had left his Luger and stiletto on board the *Noble Savage.*

He slowly lowered his hand and opened the door. He had scarcely stepped from the car when two of the men in back were on him, frisking him.

"He's clean."

They all advanced. The spokesman pointed his gun at Chandra. "You, stay in the car, don't move!"

He stuck the revolver in his belt, reached into the open car, and yanked Joanna over the side as if she were a feather.

She fell sprawling on the dust. When he yanked her up she tried to fight him. He went for her with both hands. She spun away and started running. He lunged and caught her dress, ripping it down the back as she struggled free.

"Nick!" There was shocked terror in her scream, a scream that tore through the still air. *"They want me!"*

The man grabbed her again and yanked. She turned to claw, but he stepped back and batted her hard across the mouth. Her knees sagged. He caught her around the waist, dragging her to the open door of the Citroepn. He used his knee to bounce her inside, headfirst, like a sack of laundry. Slamming the door, he came back toward the BMW.

Through it all, Carter hadn't moved. He couldn't. One long-barreled revolver was jammed in his belly, another was against his right ear.

The spokesman went directly to Chandra and leaned

over the car toward her. Carter noticed a scar running
from his scalp behind his right ear down into his collar.
When he took a grip in Chandra's hair, Carter saw that
he was missing the ring finger and the little finger on his
left hand.

"You're Chandra Braxton?"

She nodded, tight-lipped, but didn't speak.

"Tell Lloyd we've got his slut. We'll work through
you, radio only, on that barge of yours. You understand?"

She said nothing, did nothing.

"Speak, you bitch!"

"I understand."

"Good. Monitor one-eighty megs every hour on the
hour, the commercial channel. First thing, get Lloyd
here. One more thing. If you or Lloyd, or that asshole"
—he nodded at Carter—"get this to the police or leak it
to the papers, we'll kill her. You got that?"

"What do you want?" Chandra cried. "Money?"

"You contact Lloyd and monitor your radio. In time
we'll tell you what you need to know." Here he laughed
and reached into the car with his free hand. With a yank
he shredded Chandra's blouse. "Nice tits, lady, very
nice tits."

"Pig!" she snarled, and spit in his face.

The man didn't blink. He calmly spit right back in
her face. Then a gunlike object appeared in his right
hand.

Carter recognized it immediately. It was an immuni-
zation compressor. It injected a knockout punch without
the necessity of a needle.

There was a hiss as he fired it into the side of Chandra's neck. Carter felt another one just like it pressed
against his own neck.

He heard the hiss but hardly felt a thing.

Unconsciousness was almost immediate.

Carter felt as though his stomach were erupting. Making it worse was the fact that it was erupting through the top of his head. His shirt was a damp rag in the small of his back, oozing wetness.

He opened one eye, then the other, and the world slowly came into focus. He was under a eucalyptus tree. A bar of sunlight through the thick leaves played hell with his eyeballs.

He rolled his head to the side. He saw a man and a woman hovering over a groaning Chandra. The woman was bathing Chandra's face with a damp cloth from a bucket. Their faces were old, seamed, weatherworn, and fiercely Greek.

He heard a sound and rolled his head the other way. Three young men squatted nearby, staring at him. Their faces were dark, topped by mops of curly black hair. They all wore the coarsely woven clothing of working farmers.

One of them smiled. "Papa, he is awake!"

Instantly the old man was by Carter's side. "You and your lady must have passed out from the heat."

Carter's Greek wasn't fluent but it was good enough. "How is she?"

"She is awake, but—how do you say—disoriented. We found you in the road. My boys carried you up here into the shade."

Carter tried to sit up, and immediately fell back to the ground. "What . . . what time is it?"

The old man pointed at the dipping sun, now only a sliver of orange on the horizon.

Oh, God, Carter thought, they could be out of the country by now.

Again he tried to sit up. This time two of the young men jumped up to help him. Two pairs of strong hands hauled him clear to his feet. With their help he was able to stagger to Chandra.

Her eyes were open but the pupils were nearly non-existent. She did seem to focus on Carter.

"Joanna?" she croaked.

"They got her," he replied in English.

"Swell." She passed out again.

Carter turned to the two young men. "Walk me around, please."

For the next half hour the two young men obligingly walked Carter through the olive grove. When he finally had his land legs again he went down to the road.

The old truck had been pushed or driven off into the trees and abandoned. He searched it and found exactly what he expected to find: nothing. Then he studied the ground around it and the area between it and the BMW.

He came up with the same thing.

By the time he got back up the hill, Chandra was on her feet.

"How do you feel?"

"Lousy."

"Can you travel?"

"I think so. I'll just hang my head over the side."

"Do you remember?" he asked.

Her eyes came up to meet his and seemed to clear. "The instructions? Yes, I remember."

"For the time being, I think we'd better do as they say," Carter growled, and turned to the old man. "Thank you, your wife, and your sons for all your help."

The old man rolled his eyes to the sky. "You must

beware of the sun in Greece. You should put a top on
your car."

"Yeah," Carter said, "I wish I had."

He pushed a thick wad of drachmas into the old
man's protesting hand, and trundled Chandra down to
the BMW.

EIGHT

The skipper of the *Noble Savage* was Captain Timothy MacReedy. He had flaming red hair only slightly tinted, and wise eyes. He was shorter than Carter by five inches, but twenty pounds heavier. The extra weight was solid muscle distributed like a well-conditioned middleweight. Except for his potato nose and a few miscellaneous scars, his features were good.

Chandra had called him a gentle man, but outwardly quick, blunt, and tough. She also trusted him. That was why they told him everything.

"You've got them?" Carter asked. "All the instructions?"

"I do, sir."

"That frequency must be monitored twenty-four hours a day, especially on the hour."

"Yes, sir."

"The rest of the crew needn't know what's going on, except the head of your communications team."

"That will be Ryder, sir. The rest follow orders," MacReedy replied. "Will we be getting on or anchoring here for a while?"

"We'll stay here for the night," Chandra said.

"Yes, ma'am. Will that be all?"

She nodded. MacReedy made a military turn and he was out the door.

"Are you ready?" Carter asked.

"Let's do it," she replied, and picked up the phone on her desk.

A ship-to-shore overseas line had already been established. There were seven hours' difference between Athens and Washington. She was calling Senator Lloyd's office. An aide picked up on the first ring and passed Chandra immediately to the senator.

Carter picked up the extension at a nod from Chandra.

"Hello . . . Chandra?"

"Yes, Sam. Are you alone?"

"Why, yes, what is it?"

"Sam, I want you to get on another phone, a public phone."

"A public phone? But why—"

"Sam," Chandra said, "I can only scramble from this end. I want you on a public phone. Do you understand?"

"I'll call you back in twenty minutes."

Carter built a couple of drinks and they sat staring at each other for the next twenty minutes. When the phone did ring they both reached at once.

"Chandra, what the hell is going on?"

"I won't mince words, Sam. Joanna has been kidnapped."

There were several seconds of stunned silence on the other end of the line before Lloyd erupted. "*Kidnapped? My God, what for? I'm not that wealthy! What could they want?*"

"We don't know yet, Sam. They warned us not to call the police or inform the newspapers."

"But the police have to be informed!"

"Senator, this is Nick Carter. We met once at a Senate hearing on African subversives. You chaired the committee. I was a witness."

"Carter, Carter . . . yes, I seem to recall."

"I'm with a special agency connected with State, Senator. I just happened to be a guest of Ms. Braxton here on the *Noble Savage* when the abduction took place. I might be able to help."

"Help? Jesus Christ, the State Department can't help itself half the—"

"Sam," Chandra barked, "shut up. I know Carter. If anybody can help, he can."

This time the pause went on for a full minute.

"Sam?"

"I'm here. All right. What should I do?"

"Fly here to Athens tonight, Senator," Carter said. "Getting a flight shouldn't be any problem. A man by the name of Bud Corliss will meet your plane. He'll bring you to us."

"Corliss? Who's he?"

"Senator," Carter said, putting a little edge in his own voice, "Corliss is one of my people. You won't find him—or me—in any file or listed with any agency. We are nonexistent. Does that answer your question?"

"Yes, yes it does. I'll get the first flight out."

They hung up.

"What now?"

"I need to make a couple of phone calls," Carter said.

Chandra got the picture. She wasn't angry as she stood and left the room.

David Hawk, chief of AXE, was like a smoldering volcano when Carter got him on the line at last. All through the Killmaster's explanation, the other man was totally silent. The eruption took place as soon as Carter paused.

"Good God, N3, a little vacation is one thing. Getting involved with a bunch of gun merchants and a criminal operation is another!"

"I realize that, sir, but it is a senator's wife."

"True, but at times Sam Lloyd can be a damn fool. One of 'em was when he married that girl."

"What do you suggest, sir?"

"Follow it through," Hawk growled. "What else can you do? You're in too deep now. If you don't, Lloyd will start digging to find out who you are and all hell will bust loose on the Hill."

"Yes, sir," Carter said, keeping his voice controlled, low, modulated. "I'd like every section chief in the Med area alerted. Everything kept quiet, of course."

"All right. What else?"

"I'll brief Bud Corliss in Athens myself. I'm going to need all the help he can give me. I'd like everything you can get me on Zax Feeyad."

"Keep me apprised."

"I will."

"And listen, Carter, the next time you want to run off on a vacation and get laid, pick somebody a little less prone to international incidents than Chandra Braxton."

Carter didn't have to say good-bye. Hawk had hung up.

It was no secret that Hawk didn't approve of Chandra Braxton or her business. But then Hawk didn't approve of most of Carter's contacts, no matter how helpful they were on missions. AXE was a supersecret, semirenegade agency, but appropriations still had to be made to run it.

Next he called the head of AXE in Athens, Bud Corliss, and gave him the whole story.

"Chances are they've got her out of the country by now, but it's worth checking."

"Right," Corliss replied. "Got any idea who they might be?"

"Hired hands," Carter replied. "I'm sure of it. Only one of them spoke, and I'm pretty sure his English had either a Greek or a Turkish accent. He's probably still in the country."

"You're sure you don't want the authorities in on it?" Corliss asked.

"Not yet," Carter replied, "not until we know what they want. Use your clout with the airlines and try to get all incoming names."

Corliss whistled. "At this time of year that could be a big order."

"I know, but do it and then group them by country."

"I'll do my best. Anything else?"

"That's it. I'll be in touch."

Carter hung up and headed for the wheelhouse. He met Chandra halfway; she was running down the passageway.

"I was just coming to get you," she said breathlessly.

"They made contact?"

She nodded. "We taped it."

He followed her to the communications room. Three officers were on duty in the elaborate complex. From this room Chandra Braxton could keep her fingers on her world-spanning business interests twenty-four hours a day. Besides a bank of computers, there were radio and telephone connections to every major city in the world.

"This is my chief of communications, Alex Ryder. Alex, Nick Carter."

"How do you do, sir?"

Alex Ryder looked like a cross between a California beach boy and a linebacker for Scandinavian U. Carter shook his hand and winced. Under all that blond hair and good looks Carter knew that Alex Ryder was the best in the business.

"Alex knows everything," Chandra said. "I thought it best."

Carter nodded. "Any kind of a fix?"

The blond head shook from side to side. "We have a location-and-fix device programmed for both orbital navigational satellites and ground-wave transmissions. We couldn't fix on either one."

"What does that mean?" Carter asked.

"My guess is they used a small, old-style transmitter-receiver to a booster, and then bounced it our way."

"What about range?"

"Not over two hundred miles at the most."

"Could you tell if it was moving?"

"Not for sure," Ryder replied, "but there was some skip-distance in the signal. My guess would be yes."

"Then it could have come from a boat or plane," Carter said. "Let's give a listen."

Ryder flipped on the tape.

"Mrs. Braxton... Mrs. Braxton... *Mrs. Braxton*..."

There was a five-second delay and then a repeat. When the pause came again, Chandra spoke.

"This is Braxton. Go ahead."

"So far you have done well. The husband has been informed?"

"Yes, he's flying here tonight. He should arrive sometime tomorrow afternoon."

"Excellent. You will sail to Minos tonight. Anchor there in the harbor. A letter will be waiting at general delivery in the village tomorrow morning. Do you understand?"

"Quite. And Mrs. L.?"

"One second."

There was a brief pause and Joanna Lloyd's voice came on.

"Yes . . ."

"Joanna, it's Chandra."

"Yes."

"Are you all right?"

"Fine, I'm fine."

"We're doing everything we can."

"Fine."

"Is there anything you want me to tell Sam?"

The male voice returned. "We'll do the telling, Mrs. Braxton. Good night."

It was the end of the transmission.

"She sounded drunk," Chandra said.

"Or doped," Carter replied. "What about the man? Could you tell anything from his voice?"

"German or Dutch," she replied.

"Excuse me . . ." the young officer interrupted.

"Yeah?" Carter said.

"My family name was Rydeersson before my father changed it. The accent was definitely Dutch. It sounded just like my grandfather . . . the hard r's and the elongated vowels."

Carter scribbled an address on a slip of paper and handed it to Ryder. "Make a copy of the tape. Have it hand-delivered to a man named Corliss at that address.

Tell him I want a voiceprint, everything he can tell me."

"Yes, sir."

Carter headed for the hatch with Chandra right behind him.

"Should I sail?" she asked.

"Yeah. I'll join you later. I'm going to dinner."

Joanna Lloyd stepped from the shower, removed the towel from her hair and shook it out. Still wet, she took a thick robe from behind the door and belted it around her.

Carrying her drink, she entered the bedroom and sat at the vanity. She was brushing her hair when he appeared in the mirror behind her.

"Everything all right?"

"Fine," she said.

"Do you have everything you need?"

"Yes, except my freedom."

He smiled. "You will only be what you call a 'prisoner' for a few days, I assure you."

NINE

Carter didn't bother to check for a tail. He figured there was probably one there, but at this point he didn't give a damn.

He left Athens flying in the BMW and went south. When he hit the coast he turned east toward Sounion. At the foot of the Temple of Poseidon, he turned into Dimitri's.

The restaurant was a wonderful old Greek mansion, converted and modernized. It faced south and west toward the sea, and nestled in a grove of two-hundred-year-old olive trees. The trees beautifully framed the long white building against the white beach and the deep aquamarine of the sea beyond.

The interior was a Greco-Roman hybrid with marble pillars and white marble floors, accented only by strips of crimson carpet. The bar area was near the entrance, and a series of table-filled terraces gracefully spread down the side of the mountain, ending with a hedge and a sheer drop to the bay.

"You are dining this evening, sir?" The maître d' was tuxedoed with a red cummerbund and shellacked hair.

He was also about six feet five and built like an over-the-road truck.

Dimitri Adopolous liked his diners to dine peacefully.

"No, I'll just have a drink at the bar."

"Of course, sir."

"Any chance of talking to Dimitri?"

"Whom shall I say, sir?"

"Carter."

"Of course."

Carter took a dark, quiet table two terraces down and ordered ouzo.

Dimitri himself arrived with the drink. He was a massive figure with a falsely humble smile that failed to hide the intelligence in his little black eyes.

The restaurant, of course, was a toy and also a legitimate front. Dimitri was a smuggler, the biggest and the best on the Mediterranean. He was also a fixer, or broker, who bought and sold various services if the price was right. If anything was going down in Greece, Dimitri had part of the action . . . or knew who did.

"Nicholas, my friend, you're not eating?"

"Drinking," Carter replied, standing to greet the man.

They embraced, traded sloppy kisses on both cheeks, and sat. A waiter was there instantly with another glass of ouzo for his boss.

"Drinking only?" Dimitri commented with a sharp rise of one eyebrow. "It must be business."

Carter nodded. "I have a friend, female type. She was snatched this afternoon up north."

"This friend . . . ?"

"The wife of a very important American."

A cloud darkened the Greek's face and the eyes narrowed. "That is unfortunate."

Carter leaned across the table, his voice low. "Dimitri, I believe they were Greeks. At least one of them. He was the only one who spoke."

"How many?"

"Five." Carter described them and then zeroed in on the leader. "He had a scar behind his right ear down into his collar, deep and wide. Also, the little finger and the ring finger of his left hand were missing."

"Tell me more about the operation. How did it go off?"

Carter explained. "You're thinking what I'm thinking?"

Dimitri nodded. "Military training, and from the sound of it, they had inside information."

"I don't think they kept her in the country, but if I can find this man I might find out where or who they passed her off to."

Dimitri hoisted his bulk to his feet. "I will make some phone calls. It's liable to take some time."

Carter shrugged. "That's all I've got right now."

The Killmaster drank ouzo, tried to clear his mind, and drank more ouzo.

The restaurant was nearly empty by the time Dimitri returned to the table.

"It is not positive, but there's a good chance your man is Italian. At least his father was Italian. His mother was Greek. He's Calabrese, from Crotone. His name is Ugo Belladini."

"What's his sheet like?" Carter asked.

"He's a bad boy. Robbery and dope in Milan, kidnapping in Rome, twice."

"What about over here?"

"Hijacking, arms from the American military base here in Greece. He was indicted but never convicted. He was deported four years ago."

Carter chewed on a thumbnail. "It's stretching it, Dimitri."

The Greek smiled. "It's stretching it to have *two* men with these same scars, the same missing fingers, and the logical background."

Carter nodded and noticed the wide smile on the other man's face. "What is it?"

"You're in luck, my friend. Ugo's got a sister. She sings in a fisherman's club in Lovro." He looked at his watch. "It stays open until four. You've got plenty of time."

"Name?"

"Rosa. The name of the place is the Taverna Athena."

Carter started to rise and hold out his hand.

"Wait a moment, my friend," Dimitri said, his voice suddenly low. "This place is a fisherman's place. They don't like outsiders. Maybe I should send Marko with you."

Carter chewed on this for a minute. "Not with me, Dimitri. But here's what Marko can do for me."

Five minutes later Dimitri wagged a finger and the huge *maître d'* rumbled over.

"Marko, change clothes . . ."

Carter slowed at the village limits and turned toward the beach road. It was no more than a dusty lane between two rows of ramshackle houses. Every other place was a bar, most of them open-fronted with thatched roofs. Despite the hour, men sat at the outside tables drinking steadily and singing.

At the end of the street he saw a worn, hand-lettered sign ATHENA. He parked and walked. From two doors away he could hear a woman singing above the chatter

and laughter of male voices. The voice was good and
the song was Greek, all guts and tears.

He came to the end of the street. The Athena was
larger than the others, and packed. Carter squeezed his
way to a plank bar and ordered ouzo.

The woman—he assumed it was Rosa Belladini—
stood on a makeshift stage while a dark little man in
white sat behind her on an upended beer case, lightly
strumming a guitar.

She was tall, with black hair in wild disarray, olive
skin, and a full figure. Although she was not truly beautiful, she was voluptuous. And, as the only woman in
the place, she could have looked a hell of a lot worse
and still had all the attention riveted on her.

Carter sipped his ouzo. When her eyes picked him
out, they registered a new face in the place. Carter
smiled. The eyes said nothing and moved on.

She had been singing in Greek. Now she shifted to
Italian. No one seemed to notice.

There was a particularly rowdy bunch at the table
directly in front of where she stood. As Carter watched,
one of them, a big man, bare to the waist with a very
hairy torso, reached his paw toward her. With a howl of
laughter he ran his hand up under her skirt.

The woman didn't miss a note. She lifted her right
leg and sent her heel into the man's chest. He careened
back into his chair and over, his bulk hitting the plank
floor with a thud.

His companions hooted with laughter. The man on
the floor didn't think it was funny. He came up roaring
like a bull. He lunged for the platform.

His intent was obvious. Carter looked around. Not a
man in the place looked as if he wanted to stop what
was coming. Just to the right of the platform was a door.
Carter guessed it was an exit to the rear parking lot. If

he really got in trouble—mob trouble—he had a way out.

For now, he had his opening.

The hairy one was on the platform now and the chase had begun. The woman was screaming at him in two languages and clawing at his face. His big hand hooked itself in the front of her peasant blouse.

She cursed him some more and tried to pull away.

The front of the blouse ripped away and her breasts swung free. The crowd roared its approval. Carter moved toward the platform.

"You want some help?"

She gazed wide-eyed at Carter over the hulk's shoulder. The man was pawing at her breasts. She nodded.

Carter brought his knee up, hard, into the man's coccyx. The huge Greek howled with pain and whirled, his eyes blazing.

"Why don't you sit down and let the lady sing?" Carter said calmly.

Both hands came up headed for Carter's throat. The Killmaster ducked and drove his right fist into the man's belly up to the wrist. When he came down, Carter mashed his face with a knee.

The man grunted and fell like a poleaxed steer.

Carter bowed to the woman. "You sing very well. Sing." He pushed a few bills into the guitar player's shirt pocket. "Play."

The men cheered as Carter moved back to the bar and his ouzo.

The woman pushed the hairy one off the platform with her foot. Then, without trying to repair her blouse, she sang two more songs with her breasts dancing with each movement.

When she finished, she joined Carter at the bar. "Thanks."

"That happen often?"

She shrugged. "Every night. But not that bad. He's a bastard. Wants me to be his woman." She had fished a couple of safety pins from her purse and set about repairing the blouse.

Carter switched to Italian. "Can I buy you a drink?"

"Sure."

"Not here. Someplace quiet."

She studied him for a moment, then nodded. "Across the street."

She took his arm as they walked. "Rosa."

"Nick."

"What are you doing in a rathole like the Athena?"

"Looking for you."

She accepted it with a shrug.

The taverna across the street was quiet, an old folks' home. They sat at one of the secluded tables outside. Carter ordered another ouzo. Rosa asked for a beer.

"Why do you work in a place like that?"

She shrugged. "It's better than what I used to do."

"Which was?"

"A whorehouse in Athens."

"Oh."

The drinks came. "Thanks again," she said, and drank half the beer in one tip. "Why are you looking for me?"

"Your brother, Ugo."

"Oh, shit . . ."

She started to rise. Carter sat her down with a hand on her wrist. "He's in big trouble."

She snorted. "That asshole is always in big trouble." She took cigarettes from her purse and lit one.

"When was the last time you saw him?"

She drank some more beer and sighed. "You police?"

"In a way."

"American?"

He nodded. "You don't want to tell me, fine. You'll have to tell the real police."

This got her. The eyes came up flashing. Carter guessed why.

"You did time," he said.

She melted in her chair as the bones seemed to evaporate in her body. "Three years, Kampos."

"For helping your brother?"

"No, manslaughter. I killed my pimp."

Carter smiled. "He probably deserved it."

"He did. He was a bastard."

Carter took five American hundreds out of his wallet and spread them on the table in front of her. "You owe your bother more loyalty than this?"

She eyed the money hungrily and shook her head. "I don't owe him nothing."

"When?" Carter asked.

"Four days ago."

"Alone?"

"No, three other guys. They needed a quiet place to stay for two nights."

"The other three . . . were they Greek?"

"No, Italians." She lit another cigarette from the stub of the old one. "Another guy picked them up in a van."

"Was he Italian?"

"No, big guy, blond hair. He spoke English. It was funny English."

"What kind of 'funny'?"

"Hell, I don't know. I don't speak very good English myself. What did they do?"

"Something bad, very bad," Carter countered. "Was Ugo ever in the army?"

"Hell, no regular army would have him," she hooted derisively. "But he told me he did fight in a war."

"Where?"

"Somewhere down in Africa . . . Angola, I think."

"Rosa, where is he now?"

"Search me."

Carter's eyes narrowed. "You must have some idea."

Her face flushed angrily. "Man, what do you want for your five hundred?"

He sighed and stood. "You're right, I guess." He turned to leave.

"Hey. . ."

"Yeah?"

"What did they do?"

"They kidnapped a woman."

Rosa shivered visibly and stared at the money. Slowly she folded it and put it into her purse. When she spoke it was barely a whisper. "I got pregnant when I was fourteen. He was sixteen, a good boy. I loved him. We were going to get married. Ugo said it was a stain on our family's honor. The day we were supposed to get married, Ugo killed him—cut him almost in half right in front of me—and made me help him bury the body."

Carter waited.

"We were born in Crotone. Ugo has a girl friend about six miles south of the village. She has a little farm. She's a widow. Her name is Jacobelli. Luciana Jacobelli." She turned and walked away.

Carter watched her walk through the door of the Athena and then he headed for his car. Halfway there, he spotted movement coming his way from a stone wall beside the road. He reached for his Luger, then held it when he recognized Marko.

"You were right," the big man grunted. "You had a tail. This way."

Marko led him to a Fiat. A tall, blond-haired man was propped up in the passenger seat. His neck was tilted at a crazy angle.

"Sorry," Marko said with a shrug. "He had a knife and he knew how to use it. It was him or me." He handed Carter the contents of the man's pockets.

There was a well-worn passport and a wallet stuffed with a mixture of drachmas and American five-hundred-dollar bills.

The man had been a South African, Hans Veerdelph. The address was Capetown. From the last exit stamp, he hadn't been home in six years.

"Can you take care of it?"

Marko nodded. "Fish food."

Carter nodded and walked back to the BMW.

Two hours later he was in the helicopter from the *Noble Savage*, heading over the Ionian Sea toward the toe of Italy's boot.

TEN

It was dawn when the helicopter set down at the small Crotone airport. Customs, greased along with a few well-placed dollars, didn't take long.

He sent the chopper pilot back to Athens and hit a telephone.

Joe Crifasi was a stocky fireplug of a man who laughed a lot and loved booze and women. He was also mean as hell when the occasion demanded it. His territory was all of Italy, and he knew it and its natives like the back of his hand.

Carter reached Crifasi at his rented villa just outside Rome. The man had been sleeping, but he came alert the moment Carter identified himself.

"Where the hell are you, Nick?"

"Crotone, on the coast," Carter replied, and explained the situation. "I'll need a team and equipment, local boys if possible."

"No problem. We'll be there by noon, one at the latest."

"You got a driver down here I can use?"

"One sec." Carter blinked the weariness from his eyes while he waited. "Nick?"

"Yeah?"

"Polo Chappi. He's a fisherman. This time of the morning you'll catch him down at the docks. He's a good man. We can use him going in."

"See you," Carter said, and hung up.

He grabbed a cab to the docks and asked around. It didn't take long to find Chappi in a café having breakfast.

He was a middle-aged man with grizzled hair and hooded eyes set deep in his skull. His face was the color of old bronze and constantly sported a cold, sardonic smile. The eyes were black and bright as nailheads in leather. He looked like a quiet, powerful man.

All it took was a quick look at Carter's ID and the mention of Crifasi's name. The Killmaster explained what he needed in short, terse sentences and they left the café.

Aboard Chappi's boat, the man tossed Carter rough seaman's clothes. He changed and they both adjourned to a beat-up, rusty Fiat.

"You know the farm of Luciana Jacobelli?"

The man grunted that he did, and they took off in a cloud of smoke.

The house was on the top of a ravine leading down to the sea. It was large, as Italian farmhouses go, two stories with the upper bedrooms on the inland side. It rambled as if it had been built in haphazard stages, with a veranda on three sides, and two doors, front and rear.

In the rear were gardens, hedgerows, and trees that could be used for cover. Approach from the sea would be tricky, but possible under cover of darkness.

There were two cars and an old truck parked in the

drive, but Carter could see no movement inside the house.

"What do you know about the woman?" Carter asked Chappi as he peered through a pair of high-powered binoculars that the man had provided.

"Not much. She keeps to herself. Her husband was killed in prison a year or so ago. This was her parents' farm. They died two, maybe three years ago."

Carter sketched the exterior and what he could guess of the interior, and they returned to Chappi's boat.

Carter slept until Crifasi awakened him at three in the afternoon.

"Sorry it took so long."

"It's all right," Carter said. "We can't go in until dark anyway."

He was introduced to the two men Crifasi had recruited by first name only: Dino and Septi. They were both dark, taciturn men with an aura of calm deadliness about them.

Over coffee, Carter sketched the layout and the best way of entry.

"The doors are old, thick wood, and solid, here and here. Who's the explosives man?"

Septi nodded. "Me. We brought low-core plastique and synchronized detonators. If you want, I can blow them both at the same time."

"Good idea. Radio?" Carter asked, and Septi nodded. "Excellent. Crifasi and I will go in the rear. Septi, you and Dino hit the front. Polo, you're here with the sniper rifle to cover us until we're inside, and pop anybody dumb enough to dive through a window. Everybody got it?"

All heads nodded.

"What are we using?" the Killmaster asked.

"Ingrams," Crifasi replied, "and stun grenades."

"Okay," Carter said. "The woman will probably be in one of the two upstairs bedrooms, here, if she's still there. That's our first objective. We'll try to keep as many of them alive as possible, so use the grenades before you start firing. We go at dusk."

Carter left them to study the floor plans, and walked the short distance to the café. He got a mountain of coins and got a marine line to the *Noble Savage*. Chandra was summoned at once from her cabin.

"For now," Carter said, "this is just for your ears and Corliss's. Is he there?"

"Yes."

"I got a locate on the five who did the job. We go tonight. Did Lloyd arrive?"

"Yes. He's a wreck, but calm," she replied.

"The letter?" Carter asked.

"They want a meet with Lloyd in Athens."

"When?"

"Didn't say."

"No money demands?" Carter asked.

"No, just the meet. They called it a 'discussion' in the letter. I'm to give them a reply in the morning."

"How?"

"They are calling at nine, a phone booth outside a taverna here on Minos."

"Covering their ass, aren't they," Carter growled. "Put Corliss on."

"I'm here, Nick."

"What have you got?"

"The voice on the tape was a bastardized Dutch. The expert says South African. He's probably in his thirties, perhaps younger, and a heavy smoker. Maybe drinks as well."

"What about the airlines?"

"Lot of names, Nick. My office is still playing mix

and match with our files, Interpol, and the locals. Nothing yet."

"Stay on it. They've got a man in Athens, and I'm guessing he's not a local."

"You know Greece, Nick—it's like a sieve if you come in by sea. But we'll stay on it."

"See you in the morning."

Carter hung up and returned to the boat.

If they didn't want money, he wondered, what the hell did they want?

There was a light in one of the upstairs bedrooms, and a single lamp in the great room on the first floor. From his position on the rise behind the woods Carter could spot no movement inside the house. The two cars and the truck were still in the narrow drive. They hadn't been moved since the earlier reconnaissance.

With a sigh he handed the binoculars back to Polo Chappi. "Something's wrong, but I can't put a finger on it," he said.

"Yeah, too quiet," the other man grunted.

Crifasi agreed. "And they don't have anyone at the windows or outside."

"Well, "maybe they're just being careless, overconfident," Carter declared. "Let's move."

It had all been talked out a dozen times. Further words weren't needed. From now on all communication would be with hand signals.

At the first row of hedges, Chappi dropped off and went up a tree like a monkey. Dino moved away in the darkness in a flanking movement around the ridge. He would go practically to the sea and then double back in the front to join Septi after the charges were planted on the doors.

Carter checked to make sure Chappi had them covered from his roost, and then silently vaulted the gate that led into the garden. Immediately he dropped to his belly with the Ingram sweeping the house.

Crifasi came over and did the same, and then gave Septi a hand signal.

Septi came over and landed on his feet like a cat, running. His sneakers made no sound as he leaped to the porch and crouched by the door.

He was completely in shadows, but Carter could visualize him kneading plugs of the plastique into place around the lock and hinges of the door. Next would come the detonator caps. These would be linked to the tiny pulse receiver.

He saw Septi back off the veranda and wait in a crouch for a few seconds. When there was no reaction from the house, he moved like a shadow to the corner and disappeared.

Carter gave him a twenty count and nodded to Crifasi. Ten feet apart, they rushed the house. One jump took them to the veranda and they flattened themselves against the wall, the Ingrams at the ready across their chests.

The Killmaster looked up at the sky. There was a half-moon, but swirling clouds dimmed much of its illumination. Still, if anyone stepped outside for any reason, they would spot one or more of the team.

Crifasi had been mentally ticking off the seconds. When he moved the barrel of the Ingram back and forth, both he and Carter hunched down low, facing away from the door.

Septi had balanced his charges perfectly, using just enough to shatter the locks and hinges, but no more. The noise was like the single sharp crack of a high-powered rifle.

Carter and Crifasi were both on the move as the door

sagged inward. They put it on the floor with their
shoulders, and ran on over it.

They reached the large center room simultaneously,
with Septi and Dino entering from the other side.

Carter lobbed a stun grenade to the right, Crifasi to
the left. Septi and Dino bolted for the stairs, lobbing
two more into the upstairs hall as they moved.

There was no pause, no confusion. Carter checked
the kitchen and pantry. Crifasi took the downstairs bedroom.

Upstairs, they could hear the two bedroom doors
burst with well-aimed kicks directed against the locks.

Then silence.

Crifasi and Carter met back in the center of the main
room, both wearing puzzled frowns. Septi appeared at
the top of the stairs.

"Up here."

Carter led the way and followed Septi's nod into the
larger of the two bedrooms, Crifasi right behind him.

"Jesus," Crifasi moaned.

"Shit," Carter growled.

There were five of them, four men and one woman.
They had been lined up against one wall of the bedroom
and executed, firing-squad fashion. Now their bodies
seemed to grotesquely entwine around each other in
death.

Carter checked. The woman wasn't Joanna Lloyd.

"Three minutes. Search every room and take anything that might be proof that the American woman was
here."

Carter knelt by the bodies, tugging a plastic bag from
his belt. He stripped the men of any identification he
could find and rejoined the others below.

"Arsenal in one of the closets," Septi said, "but that's
it."

"I've got telephone bills for the last two months," Crifasi added. "That might help."

Dino had come up blank.

"Let's get out of here," Carter hissed.

At the boat, they split up. Crifasi, Septi, and Dino kept on going for Rome in the van. Polo Chappi cast off and he and Carter headed for open sea across the Gulf of Taranto. By midnight they would be in the heel of the boot at Casarano. There was a small airfield there where Carter could get a light plane charter for Athens.

The stakes, he thought, were high, and whoever was setting them meant to win.

ELEVEN

The chopper picked Carter up in Athens, and a half hour later it was setting down on the fantail of the *Noble Savage*. Chappi had taken the tiller himself all the way across the gulf, so Carter had been able to get some sleep. Even at that he looked—and felt—as if he had been on his feet for days.

Dawn was just breaking over the horizon, but Bud Corliss and Chandra were up and alert.

"Anything new?" Carter asked, alighting from the chopper.

"The file on Feeyad is in," Corliss declared. "Other than that, it's quiet."

Carter handed over the plastic bag full of the personal stuff he had taken from the bodies, along with the passport Marko had taken from Hans Veerdelph, and the telephone bills from the farm.

"Do a check on these. They're all bad boys, so it shouldn't be hard to find something on them. Also, check the long-distance calls on those bills."

Corliss held up the bag. "Where did these come from?"

Carter told them. Chandra got a little pale, but Corliss just shrugged and headed for the waiting chopper.

"They were all dead?" Chandra asked with a swallow.

"Executed."

"You look like hell," she said, wanting the subject changed.

"I got a little sleep. Get Lloyd up, will you? As soon as I grab a shower I want to talk with him."

"I'll send you some coffee."

"Thanks," Carter said. "And send Ryder around with the file on Feeyad."

He took a hot shower, then ran the water ice-cold for the last few minutes. He shaved, dressed in lightweight clothes, and dropped into a comfortable chair with a cup of strong Greek coffee and the life of Zax Feeyad.

What there was of it that Carter didn't know, he could have guessed. Feeyad had his sticky fingers in several dozen pies, and while a lot of them were shaky or shady, there was nothing showing that would stand up in an international court.

The last three pages were financial. Feeyad was loaded. He owned homes in Algeria, France, Italy, and Morocco, as well as apartments in most major cities. He also had a private plane on twenty-four-hour call, and a yacht that came close to the *Noble Savage* in opulence.

There wasn't a mention of any holdings in Namibia, but Feeyad had a ton invested in various mining interests in South Africa itself.

Chandra rapped lightly on the door and entered. "The senator is on his way to my office. I've ordered coffee and breakfast served there for the two of you."

"Thanks. You suppose you could call in a few I.O.U.s in the Caymans, Switzerland, maybe South Africa?"

"I can try," she replied.

He handed her the file. "Read between the lines on those investments. See how many of them dovetail into Namibia. You sold him your stock. Chances are he's bought from someone else."

He walked along the passageway and stepped into Chandra's private domain. It was part office, part study, and everything but feminine. Massive, durable furniture in fine leather inside teak walls.

Breakfast had already been served on a small, round conference table. When Carter entered, Senator Sam Lloyd sat staring into a cooling cup of coffee. He stood as Carter approached.

"Senator, I'm Nick Carter."

"I vaguely remember you . . . sorry."

"It's been a few years."

Lloyd eased back into his chair and Carter poured coffee for himself.

Lloyd was a lean, gray-haired man who wore rimless glasses that he was constantly pushing back up his nose. He wore a stern, dark-blue business suit that seemed incongruous on the yacht. Other than the magazine-perfect clothes, he looked like hell.

"Have you made any headway at all?" he asked, raising weary eyes to Carter.

"Some," the Killmaster said, preferring at this point to keep the man in the dark.

"And you still have not informed the authorities?"

"Until we know exactly what they want, I think it best to keep everything to ourselves. Also, in some ways, we have a larger range of operations than any one police force. Tell me, Senator, do you know a man named Zax Feeyad?"

The senator thought for a moment. "Vaguely, only by reputation. Does he have anything to do with this?"

"I hope to find out." Carter paused. "Tell me about your wife, Senator."

"What?"

"Your wife. Tell me about her. Where did you meet?"

"I don't see—"

"It could mean a great deal," Carter said, almost harshly. "I'd like to know . . . everything."

A little flush crept up between the senator's collar and ears, but he started talking. "We met in London, almost four years ago. We've been married a little less than three years."

"Then she's English?"

"Yes."

"How did you meet her? Were you introduced?"

"Yes, at an embassy reception. I don't remember who actually introduced us."

"Joanna—Mrs. Lloyd—is English by birth?"

"Yes. She was born in a small village in Cornwall."

"Were you happy?" Carter asked bluntly.

"Yes."

Lloyd looked away, the answer too fast. Carter leaned forward, his elbows on the table. "Senator, Chandra has told me about your wife's infidelities. It was necessary."

Lloyd started to get irate, but crumpled instead. For a moment Carter thought he might cry. The Killmaster sipped his coffee, giving the man time.

"About two weeks ago I had an important conference in New York. I was to have been gone a week, but I came back to Washington from New York a day early. She . . . she was in bed with a young man. It's my fault, really. I've spent so little time with her. She's young. She needs to do things, see people. When we were married I never dreamed that my career would stand in the way . . . it's difficult for her."

"Did she have other affairs," Carter probed, "that you know about?"

"Only once, a few months after we were married."

"In Washington?"

"No, London. There was a conference on human rights. I was one of the speakers. It was quite by accident that I found out. I had an hour or so. I went shopping, in Harrods. I saw her with this young man. I was angry, of course, but then I thought it could be just an innocent luncheon, a chance meeting. I followed them when they left."

"And?"

Lloyd's jaw tightened. "They went to a cheap hotel in Piccadilly. They didn't come out for nearly three hours."

"You faced her with it?" Carter asked.

"Yes, that night. She cried, became hysterical. She told me that the young man was an old school chum of hers. She was bored. She begged my forgiveness and promised it would never happen again."

"And it didn't, for two years?"

"No, I'm sure of it."

"All right, Senator, now tell me about Namibia and your U.N. lobby."

Lloyd glanced up sharply. "Good God, Carter, what's that got to do with my wife's kidnapping?"

"I don't know, Senator, maybe nothing . . . maybe a great deal."

Lloyd had come halfway out of his chair. Now he settled back with a sigh. "As I'm sure you know, we have several sanctions on South Africa. I want another one. I want them out of Namibia so that the country can hold free elections. In a nutshell, that's it."

"How's it going?"

"Tight. One vote could swing it either way. But I've been doing a great deal of work. With luck and some tenacity, I think I can swing it."

"When is the final vote?"

"A week from today."

Carter thought about this for a moment. "What kind of effect will your being here, away from the action, have on the vote?"

The man shrugged. "Hard to say. It could have a great deal of effect."

Carter stood. "Thank you, Senator. Oh, one more thing . . ."

"Yes?"

"The young man in London that your wife met that day? Do you think you could recognize him again?"

Now the color completely drained from his face. "Yes, I would recognize him. I could never forget him."

"Thank you, Senator."

Carter went to the communications room just aft of the bridge. The tall blond, Ryder, was on duty. "Get me a ship-to-shore, Washington. Here's the number. And open me another line to Bud Corliss."

"Yes sir."

He had to have the call rerouted through the night duty officer to Ginger Bateman's Georgetown apartment.

"Do you know what time it is here?" she huffed when she recognized his voice.

"Wee hours," Carter replied, "but this is important. I want a background check on Joanna Lloyd."

"There's one on file, security clearance, everything. She's a senator's wife, Nick."

"I know. But I want to go deeper. Get MI5 in London in on it. Turn over rocks—see if there are any discrepancies."

"Okay," she groaned. "By the way, did you get my memo on Pavel?"

"No. You mean Pavel in Germany?"

"That's right, Pavel in Germany who got blown away. Corliss probably has it."

"Give it to me briefly."

"You were right. There was very little in the papers Pavel handed over. But when the info request came in on that South African, Hans Veerdelph, I remembered that that name was mentioned in one of the papers."

"Damn," Carter hissed, "I must have missed it. In what way?"

"Veerdelph was a mercenary in Angola and Namibia, evidently free-lance. Seems he infiltrated some Italians into the rebel cause down there, passed them off as Italian Red Brigades. By the time he pulled them out and sent them home, he had scored a yard-wide coup."

"Who did he work for?"

"Private. An outfit called Aadlon International. Moscow was seriously thinking of a sanction, but they couldn't find him."

"Ginger, you're a sweetheart," Carter said. "Get me the Joanna Lloyd information as soon as possible."

He hung up and Ryder made the second connection. Corliss was on the line.

"I've got all kinds of stuff for you, Nick."

"Hold it for now," Carter said. "I'll be in by noon or shortly after. When you send the chopper for us, put an identikit man in it."

"Will do. That it?"

"For now."

Carter hung up and found Chandra at his elbow.

"It's time to go ashore and take our little phone call," she said.

It was obvious to Carter that Chandra Braxton was getting tired of playing go-between.

Carter didn't blame her. He was getting tired of playing games in the dark himself.

Two seamen flipped fenders out to protect the gleaming point on the hull of the launch. Another sailor was forward and another aft. When the helmsman hit reverse, they pulled the craft in and tied up neatly.

Carter stepped to the pier and gave Chandra a hand.

"It's this way."

He followed her across the street and into a narrow alley that ran up the hills between whitewashed houses.

"That's it, Popy's."

They took a table outside and ordered coffee. The pay phone above their heads rang at exactly nine o'clock.

Chandra fastened the suction cup of the recorder and picked up the receiver. Carter remained seated and inserted an earplug with a wire to the recorder.

At a nod from Carter, Chandra spoke into the instrument. "Yes?"

"Mrs. Braxton."

"This is she."

"So far, so good, Mrs. Braxton. No authorities, no newspapers. I commend you."

"Just what the hell do you want?" she hissed.

"For now, merely your cooperation. Day after tomorrow, at five sharp, I want the senator to be waiting in the offices of your Athens attorney."

"Pappas?" Chandra murmured.

"That's right. He is to have a car outside the building available to him as well."

"How long is this going to go on?" she snapped into the receiver.

There was a mirthless chuckle from the other end of the line. "As long as we want it to, Mrs. Braxton. As your American friend, Carter, would say, have a nice day."

Carter made a wry face as the line went dead. Chandra released the recorder and sat down.

"What do you think?" she sighed.

"I think," he replied, "that they are eating up time, even wasting it. It's just a question of whether we find out why before they eat up all they need."

The identikit man was a dapper little Greek with Interpol named Demontos. He didn't know the story and he didn't want to. He owed Bud Corliss a favor or two, and he was repaying.

True to his word, Senator Lloyd remembered well the face of the man who had been his wife's London lover. But it took its toll as he worked with Demontos. The coat was off, the tie pulled down, and sweat beaded his face.

The Greek had a sketch pad fastened to a portable easel. His fingers flew as Lloyd picked out pieces of facial characteristics from a nearby box. The box held every feature of the human face, down to a single nostril. Warts, moles, and birthmarks were even represented.

Unable to wait in Athens, Corliss had flown out on the chopper with Demontos. While the two men worked over the sketch, narrowing the nose or broadening the forehead, Corliss and Carter moved to the far end of the room.

"The woman was Luciana Jacobelli. One of the men was Ugo Belladini. Another was Alberto Salmona. The last two were brothers, Guido and Carlo Marlotti. They all had records, even the woman."

"I expected that," Carter muttered. "What else do we know about them?"

"They'd been out of the country for the past few years. For a year they were laborers in South Africa. Then they disappeared for about six months and surfaced again with the rebels in Namibia."

"Training?" Carter asked.

Corliss nodded. "It would figure. They raised hell for nearly two years, betraying rebel bases and passing information to this Veerdelph character, then they went underground again."

"And resurfaced in Italy?"

"No. At least not for a year. During that time they worked security for this Aadlon outfit."

Carter chewed his lip. "So far, it's fitting together. Veerdelph engineered the snatch, using Ugo Belladini and the other three. The question is, who hired Veerdelph?"

"It would stand to reason that it was Aadlon," Corliss offered. "Can we put Aadlon together with Feeyad?"

"Let's go see," Carter growled.

As they walked toward the bridge, Corliss had an additional thought. "It's probably too late to help, but my man in the Greek ESA gave me the name of a smuggler who works Crotone regularly. He's got a good-sized boat. He might be the man who got the Italians in and out."

"We'll check it out," Carter said.

Chandra was at the computers. She was perspiring almost as much as the senator.

"Anything?" Carter asked as he entered the room.

She shook her head and sighed. "I've twisted Aadlon into a pretzel, straightened it out, and twisted again.

They are basically a trading company with almost everything in oil and mining shares. I did learn one thing, though, that you might find interesting: most of their investments are in Namibia."

Carter's ears immediately perked. "How big?"

"Nearly a billion. But a lot of it is short."

"Anything that might tie Aadlon to Feeyad?"

"Not a damn thing, Nick. If he controls Aadlon, he's got it so well hidden I can't dig it out. And I know every trick in the book."

Carter thought for a moment. "Can you get me a list of the company officers?"

"That I can do."

She went back to work. Carter and Corliss returned to the belowdeck's office.

"How's it going?"

"It's as good as I can get it," Lloyd replied.

"I can improve it a little," Demontos said. He went to work with fine-haired brushes and then an airbrush. Asking questions of Lloyd, the Greek added tint to hair, skin tone, and eyes.

"That's close," Lloyd exclaimed at last, "damn close."

Demontos held the finished sketch in front of him, eyeing it critically. "It will be even closer if I can get back to Athens and put it through a physiognomy computer."

"All I have to do is pack," Carter said, heading for his cabin.

The name of the smuggler who worked Crotone regularly was Gus Thanos. Carter found him in an ugly little taverna near the commercial docks. The place was as dark as a hole and smelled like a toilet.

Thanos was nursing a glass of ouzo at a corner table.

Carter slid into a chair across from him without announcing himself. Thanos glanced up darkly, his pupils foggy, his mouth slack with drink. He was as broad as the table, with dark hair hanging into his face and a deep scar on the right side of his neck.

"You want something, man?"

"Maybe take a boat ride," Carter said. "Go fishing . . . at night."

The blurred eyes narrowed and managed to focus. "You got someplace special in mind?"

"In the gulf . . . say, off Crotone?"

The eyes flashed. "You police? Leave me alone."

"I'm not the police."

"Go away. What do you want with me?"

Carter leaned close across the table, his voice a whisper. "A few days ago you picked up a party of bad boys at a farm south of Crotone. You brought them over, and probably took them back . . ."

"You're talkin' shit. I don't . . . agggg!"

Carter had reached under the table and grabbed a handful of the Greek's crotch with his right hand. As he spoke, he squeezed and twisted.

"There are two ways we can do this, Gus . . . hard, or easy."

"Bastard! Agggg . . ."

With his left hand Carter dropped a pile of bills on the table. Thanos's face still showed pain, but now there was some greed as well in the eyes as he mentally counted the bills.

"Want to talk, Gus?"

"Let go my balls, man." There were tears in his eyes now.

Carter released him. Grubby hands scooped the money into a pile and the pile went into his grubby jacket. He glanced over his shoulder to make sure the bartender hadn't seen the transaction.

"Okay, yeah, I pick up Belladini and three other guys at his woman's place. I bring 'em over to Lavro and dump 'em off."

"What about the return ride?"

"Three days later they meet me, I take 'em back. No big deal."

"In Lavro?"

"No, up the coast, Parnassos."

"What time?" Carter asked.

"Time? Hell, I don't know."

"What time did you meet them, Gus?" Carter leaned forward again and tapped the man's knee.

"All right, all right." He rubbed his forehead and frowned in concentration. "Let's see, it was afternoon . . . maybe about two, three."

"What was it, Gus, two or three?"

"Two, it was closer to two."

Carter lit a cigarette. Two o'clock. That meant Ugo and his helpers went right from the snatch to Thanos's boat.

"How did you know where to pick them up, Gus?"

The man shrugged. "I get a call here, maybe about ten o'clock that morning, tellin' me where to go."

"How was the first contact made?"

"Belladini's woman. She comes here and makes the deal."

Carter smiled. It was coming together. "How many went back to Crotone?"

"Four, what the hell do you think? I bring four over, I take four back."

Carter rose and leaned over the other man. "You earned your drachmas, Gus. Forget you ever saw me."

The Greek snorted. "With pleasure, man."

Carter exited into the sunlight and hailed a cab. "The airport," he said, and checked his watch.

He had about an hour before the flight left for Johannesburg.

Christopher Boulda lifted the phone on the first ring. *"Ja?"*

"I am at the Athens airport. The American, Carter, just boarded a flight to Johannesburg."

"Thank you." Boulda replaced the phone and turned to Zax Feeyad. "Carter took a flight to Johannesburg. He's digging."

Feeyad nodded and removed a cigar from his fat lips. "Chandra Braxton has a great deal of power, many contacts. With her help he may be able to put it all together."

"What do you think?"

"Eliminate him," Feeyad replied. "Get in touch with Carl. Tell him to use Copek. Use the fax machine, get a picture at once to Carl."

The door behind Feeyad opened and Joanna Lloyd in a tiny bikini walked into the room.

"How much longer do we have to stay cooped up here?" she whined. "Eat, sleep, swim . . . I'm bored to tears!"

Boulda stood and kissed her lightly on the lips. "Just a few more days, darling. And then the man is ours."

TWELVE

The landing was slow and easy, the wheels settling gingerly on the tarmac. It had been a seven-hour flight and Carter had used it to get some much-needed sleep.

He shrugged into his jacket and remained seated until nearly all the passengers were off, then he stood up and fell in at the tail end of the line moving down the aisle.

At customs he declared that he was not carrying heroin, marijuana, firearms, or fresh fruit. A young officer checked his passport against a subversives list, and passed him to another, older officer.

"The reason for your visit, sir?"

"Sightseeing, maybe some fishing."

"And how long will you be with us?"

Carter shrugged. "A few days."

His passport and a typed list of "Dos and Don'ts in South Africa" were handed to him with a smile.

"Enjoy, sir."

He took a cab the ten miles from Jan Smuts International into downtown Johannesburg and the Casa Mia Hotel. Quickly he checked in and went down to the dining room. He barely made it before the kitchen closed.

With a good steak in his belly, he moved across the lobby to the lounge. A trio played jazz on a small stage, and the place was packed. Carter felt he could have blown smoke rings from the exhaled atmosphere. The lighting was dim and the couples on the dance floor seemed to be standing still.

He managed to squeeze himself into a place near the bar and order a cognac. He leaned his back against the stool and turned to examine the crowd. It was difficult to see in the hazy gloom, but there was no mistaking the copper-red hair.

Chandra had said:

"You can't miss her . . . very tall, almost six feet, thin, with long, copper-red hair. She's Baals's secretary. Her name is Inez. She'll wait for you in the lounge of the Casa Mia."

Inez was talking to a man and it looked as though the conversation wasn't going well.

Carter pushed away from the bar, carrying his glass, and moved through the crowd toward her. The closer he came, the more it appeared that she wasn't getting along with the man. He appeared to be one of those creeping conversationalists. He kept moving toward her as he talked, and she, in turn, kept backing up. She backed into Carter just as he was circling two people to reach her.

"Inez!" Carter said. "I thought I had missed you!"

There was only a second's hesitation as she mentally went over the description and digested the accent.

The smile was wide, showing good, strong, white teeth. "Nick, darling!" She touched her cheek to his and ran her arm through his, then turned a melting stare on the talker.

The man quickly muttered something and moved away through the crowd.

"Bloody pest," she whispered. "Any woman alone and his type thinks her panties are automatically soaked. Did you get checked in all right?"

"I did."

"Let's have a drink in your room."

She tightened her hold on his arm and guided him from the lounge and across the lobby to the elevators.

Inez was a take-charge woman.

In the room, Carter mixed two drinks and she dived into the oversize purse she carried.

"Mrs. Braxton sent along the message that she still has not made a connection with Aadlon. She said you would know what that meant."

"I do," Carter said, moving onto the sofa beside her. "Anything else?"

"There are three officers in the company. The CEO is Christopher Boulda, chief accountant is Nils Zefsheem, and the executive secretary is Hulda Preeva. Here are their personal addresses and the offices of Aadlon."

"Here in Johannesburg?" Carter asked, looking over the list.

"Yes. So far, we have found nothing on any of them through the regular channels. We are still working on it. Veerdelph was a little easier. He has an extensive record with the South African intelligence service."

She put that file on the table and topped it with a rectangular wooden box. Carter opened it. Resting on red felt was a 9mm Gilsenti automatic, two extra seven-shot clips, and a half-choke silencer.

"There is also an American AR-17 with one hundred spare rounds in the trunk of the car. It's a Mercedes 300 four-door sedan. The license number is RAW-1014L.

It's dark blue, parked in aisle Four in the hotel's underground garage."

"And the fragmentation grenades?" Carter asked.

"Six of them, also in the trunk." She glanced at him with a grin. "Are you planning to start a war in South Africa, Mr. Carter?"

He smiled. "Not if I can help it. Is the car clean?"

She nodded. "It's registered to a dead man in Capetown. Here are papers in his name in case you can't leave the country by proper channels."

"Thank you," Carter said, "you're much more efficient than I have a right to expect. Does your boss have access to the Department of Immigration . . . motor vehicles, things like that?"

Inez smiled. "Mr. Baals has a great many contacts, yes."

Carter passed over the composite picture of Joanna Lloyd's London lover. "See if you can put a name to that."

She glanced at the picture and nodded. "We'll do everything we can. Will that be all for tonight? My husband is waiting."

Quickly, Carter scanned the file on Hans Veerdelph and came up with the name of an old girl friend. "This Crolla Snyder—get me particulars and whereabouts on her if you can. Veerdelph keeps popping up. So far he's the only name that connects with everything."

"I'll have it for you by tomorrow."

"Thank you again."

He saw her out the door, built himself a nightcap, and returned to the folders on the coffee table. Over the next two hours, he memorized names, addresses, phone numbers, and the complete file on Hans Veerdelph. When he was sure he had everything word-perfect, he burned it all in a metal wastebasket and flushed the ashes.

In bed, he set his mental alarm for six in the morning, and immediately fell asleep.

"Bruno?"

"*Ja.*"

"It's Carl. Hope I didn't awaken you."

"I was awake. What is it?"

"We have business. I am in the lobby."

"Come up."

Carl hung up and entered the elevator. He was a tiny man, barely over five feet tall, with curly black hair, gleaming capped teeth, and blue eyes that looked cold even when he smiled. He was forty-five years old and prided himself on looking thirty.

As a youth in London he had wanted a career in the Foreign Service. By the time he was twenty he had changed his mind. He had decided that he wanted a career as a millionaire.

The opportunity to achieve this goal arose in a most unlikely way. He learned that a dear aunt of his, Carl's only living relative, carried an insurance policy on herself of two hundred thousand pounds. He was the beneficiary.

For six months Carl planned the woman's murder and searched until he found the right man for the job, an Indian named Ajeeb.

The death was perfect, an accident. Carl collected the insurance money and his career was launched. For two years he used only Ajeeb, but then, as his client list grew, he found it necessary to expand his operation. At the present time Carl had twelve seasoned assassins in his employ. Of those, the most ruthless was Bruno Copek.

The door was answered on the first knock. The men did not shake hands. Copek jerked his chin and Carl entered the apartment.

The place looked like a boar's cave. Carl knew that it usually did. Once a month a colored was brought in to shovel it out.

Copek shoved several newspapers, magazines, empty beer cans, and articles of clothing from a chair and motioned Carl to sit. From the pile of clothing Carl extracted a bra with cups large enough to encase two American footballs.

"This couldn't be for human use," Carl commented dryly.

Copek giggled. "I like 'em like that."

"Poor thing," Carl muttered. "She must walk bent over like an elderly lady with osteoporosis."

Copek scowled. "What you mean? I don't have it with no diseased old wimmen." He grabbed the bra and dropped it in a wastebasket already seven-eighths full. "I put her away in the shithouse. She can't hear. What you got?"

Carl meticulously fitted a cigarette into a black holder. "A hit . . . very heavy."

"Police?"

"No, government. You'll probably have to disappear for a few months afterward. You'll be compensated extra."

"How much?"

"Ten thousand," Carl replied, blowing a perfect smoke ring.

"Pounds?"

"Of course." Carl opened his briefcase and passed the other man a thick envelope. "It's all there, including the bonus. The name is Carter. Here is a description and a photograph."

"Is he here in Capetown?"

"No, Johannesburg. He got in tonight, checked into the Casa Mia. You should be there early in the morning to spot him."

"How you want it done?"

Carl shrugged. "The quickest way possible."

Copek grinned like a wolf. "Okay if it's messy?"

"Quite," Carl replied. "In fact my client would prefer that it not look like an accident."

Copek cackled out loud. "Shit, I'll make it look like he ran into a fucking Panzer division."

Carl stood. "You have the number to call when the job is completed."

"*Ja.*"

Carl moved to the door, looked once more at the mess that was the room, made a face, and let himself out.

Bruno Copek walked through the bedroom toward the bath, letting the robe trail to the floor behind him.

His neck was as thick as a post, heavy slabs of muscle ran across his shoulders, and the slightest movement made ripples under his rather pale skin that never tanned. His T-shirt must have been at least a size 50, and his rather long arms bulged above the elbow; his wrists were three inches wide. In a suit he looked big but ordinary; in just trousers and a T-shirt he looked like an ape. He had almost colorless blue eyes that looked unfocused, or as though they had a cast.

By the time he reached the bathroom door he was naked. A brunette with proportions that almost matched his sat on the closed toilet smoking a cigarette.

"Can I come out now, luv?"

"Yeah, get your things together and get your ass outta here."

"You mad at me, luv?"

"I got business. Be outta here when I get outta the shower." He reached and squeezed one of her melonlike breasts hard. "And this time make sure all my goddamned money stays in my goddamned wallet. Got it?"

"I learned my lesson, luv," the woman said, blinking and drawing away. She had. She would never have believed a woman could survive such a beating until she had.

Bruno stalked toward the shower, chest out, grinning. Damn, he thought, good to work again. It didn't pay for a man to be idle for too long, makes you develop bad habits.

He showered quickly and ran a razor over his surprisingly spare beard, carefully lotioned and powdered himself, then combed his thick blond hair. He slipped into a short-sleeved white sport shirt, blue slacks, thick white socks and custom-made cordovan loafers, then a sports jacket.

He loaded his pockets with money clip, change, wallet, knife, handkerchief, and keys, then tucked an automatic pistol with oversize grips inside his waistband. He rubbed his crotch and grinned at himself in the mirror above his dresser, then turned and unlocked the closet. From it he took two aluminum cases. These he put in a larger bag with his clothes and toiletries.

At the phone he dialed a number from memory.

"Hello?"

"Chaka, Bruno. You gassed up?"

"Always."

"I got to go to J'burg tonight."

"No problem."

"I'll need a car up there, clean."

"No problem."

"See you in an hour."

"No problem."

Bruno Copek turned out the lights and made sure the door was double locked when he left.

Crime was getting to be a problem, even in Cape-town.

THIRTEEN

After a huge breakfast, Carter was on the road by seven the following morning. His first stop was to check the suburb where Hulda Preeva lived. It was an upper-middle-class neighborhood with row after row of new apartment houses. The executive secretary of Aadlon lived in one of the more expensive buildings. There was no doorman, but the front door was locked.

Carter moved across the street, lit a cigarette, and window-shopped while he waited.

It was twenty minutes before a woman approached the door, heavily laden with groceries. Carter flipped his cigarette and hurried across the street. She was trying to juggle paper bags and retrieve a key from her purse at the same time.

"Here, let me help you."

"Oh, thank you."

Through the glass he spotted PREEVA 8-B.

He punched the button for the eighth floor the moment he got in the elevator. "*Your* floor?"

"Five."

At five he handed her packages back to her and held the door.

On the eighth floor it took him exactly twenty seconds to pick the lock and let himself into Hulda Preeva's apartment. He pulled on a pair of thin surgical gloves and went to work.

The apartment was five rooms full of antiques, silver, quality linens, and several thousand dollars' worth of fitted drapes. Hulda Preeva had good, expensive tastes, and obviously the money to indulge them.

It took over an hour, but by the end of that time he was pretty sure he'd found a few more pieces to the puzzle. Most of it was gleaned from letters and a family scrapbook.

He copied down names and addresses, and lifted two snapshots from the family photo album. When he was sure everything was as it had been, he left.

Back in the car, he headed across the city to Herman Eckstein Park. The accountant, Nils Zefsheem, lived in a huge old colonial overlooking the park. The neighborhood was exclusive and the house in excellent shape.

Like Hulda Preeva, Nils Zefsheem didn't want for money, even though his only client as an accountant was Aadlon International, who seemed to exist for no other reason than the acquisition of shaky stock.

The house was hugged by bushes and blossoming flowers, and was separated from neighboring houses by a three-foot-high rough-stone wall. Carter went up the flagstone walk between rows of flame-bright tulips. Before he had a chance to knock, the front door was opened by a chubby guy about twenty-five years old. He had a round, baby face with rosy cheeks and a small nose made to seem smaller by the bulges of flesh on his cheeks.

"Yes?" There were several *s*'s on the end of the word.

"Herr Zefsheem?"

"Oh, no. Nils is at the office. What do you want?"

Carter flipped his wallet open and then closed it as the little man blinked. "City Planning, sir. Could I talk to you for a moment?"

"Of course. Please come in."

In Carter's mind there was little doubt about this relationship. Carter followed him down a narrow hall and into an airy study.

"Tea?" the young man asked with a smile.

"Thank you," Carter said, smiling back.

"Only a minute."

He was gone five. In that time Carter found the location of a wall safe and a paid telephone bill in the top drawer of the desk.

The rotund little man returned and poured. "What are they going to do now?"

"Not a great deal," Carter replied. "It's just time to trim the jacaranda trees along the street again, and we always like to inform the homeowners."

"Well, I must say it's about time."

Carter drank his tea and got out as fast as he could before he got raped.

The next stop was a high-rise near the center of the city on Holland. This one not only had a doorman but a burly security guard.

"Help you, sir?"

"Perhaps," Carter said, adopting a thick British accent. "Looking for a chap, Fusten. Seems to have moved."

"Sorry, sir," the guard replied. "I've been here since the building was erected, and I don't think we've ever had a tenant by that name."

"Oh, dear, probably have the wrong address."

Christopher Boulda lived in the penthouse. This one, Carter thought, wouldn't be so easy to crack. But then he might not have to. . . .

In a pay phone he dialed the number Inez had listed as Boulda's home phone.

"Yes?"

"Herr Boulda, please."

"He not here."

"Oh. Could I reach him at the office?"

"He out of town. You call back." The line went dead.

Carter drove until he found a men's clothing store, where he bought two cheap suits. Three doors away he bought a duck-billed hat and a pair of blue coveralls. At a drugstore he bought a pair of dark, wraparound sunglasses, two thick cigars, and a blank name tag.

Back in the car, he put the coveralls on a hanger between the two cellophane-covered suits. He removed his coat, rolled his sleeves to mid-bicep, and put on the hat and glasses.

Then he drove to the Golden City building and parked in the underground garage.

Bruno Copek parked across the street where he could see the dark blue Mercedes, and shook his head.

This man was crazy. What was he doing? At the rate he was moving he would never stop long enough to take a hit. Twice that morning Copek had thought he was headed out of the city. He had even taken the shotgun out of the aluminum case and assembled it, just in case. There were a half-dozen lonely stretches outside J'burg where he could have pulled up beside Carter, rolled the shotgun over his window, and taken the man out.

But he had headed, every time, right back into the city.

Now Copek eyed the Mercedes hungrily. There were seven pounds of plastique in the other aluminum case. Should he take a chance and wire the car?

No, he decided, too much foot traffic in the garage.

He would wait.

Eventually, this Carter had to light someplace.

Carter checked the building's register. Aadlon International was on the sixth floor. There were nine other companies on the sixth floor. The legal firm of Johannsen, Markson, and Brunel occupied the entire tenth floor.

There was a huge lobby on the ground floor, furnished in modernistic style, with a large curved reception desk. The blonde behind the desk was modernistic as well.

Carter looked around as he walked over to the desk. There were two uniformed men sitting in chairs to the left. They both glanced at him casually, then went back to reading their magazines. He switched his gaze back to the blonde. She looked even better at close range.

"Herr Brunel, tenth floor."

"Do you have an appointment?" she countered.

Carter shook the cellophane-covered suits. "Delivery."

"Just a minute," she murmured. She picked up one of the phones on her desk and pushed a button on it. "There's a delivery down here for Herr Brunel." She waited a minute. "All right." She replaced the phone and looked up at Carter. "Take the elevator to ten. Herr Brunel's secretary will take them."

"Thank you."

He punched ten. When it hit the floor he let the doors open and close, then hit nine. There was no maintenance closet on nine. He found one on eight.

He dumped the suits and pulled on the coveralls. He scrawled a name he couldn't pronounce on the tag, then pinned it to the breast pocket.

Everything he needed was in the closet. He filled a bucket with warm water and added enough ammonia to make his eyes water. Bucket in one hand, squeegie in the other, and rags hanging out of his pocket, he headed for six.

ARNOLD J. LEFFTIMEER IMPORTS AND EXPORTS was the first stop. It was a one-man office with a secretary. The secretary was a tired fifty with gray hair behind a tiny desk with a single no-button phone. She was reading a novel and scarcely looked up when Carter entered.

"Windows."

She nodded and kept reading. Carter went to work. He timed it so he finished at eleven-thirty, and moved next door to Aadlon.

It was a three-office setup and pretty bare: three desks, three chairs, a few filing cabinets, and a potted plant.

A nameplate on the front desk read HULDA PREEVA. The woman behind the desk was in her thirties, petite with sharp, aristocratic features and ivory-colored skin. She was wearing a delicate peach-colored dress with embroidered mountains, trees, and streams on the skirt.

Her expression, when she looked up at Carter, looked as if she had eaten wormwood and gall.

"Windows."

"Today?"

Carter shrugged. "Just do what they tell me."

She cursed under her breath and motioned to her left.

Through the open door to the office to her right, Carter could see a man with salt-and-pepper hair brushed back in stiff bristles. He was wearing a blue suit and white shirt. His collar was open, sweaty and stained, and the dark red tie, pulled into a tight knot, hung four or five inches below the collar button. The eyes were bloodshot and watery as though they were terribly strained. He looked harassed.

Carter waved. The man scowled and went back to work pounding the keyboard of a computer.

In the office, Carter poured another good hit of ammonia into the bucket, rubbed the tears from his eyes, and went to work.

Just before noon he moved into Nils Zefsheem's office.

It didn't take long. By twelve-fifteen the man's eyes were burning like fire. He signed out of the computer and stalked from the office.

"Hulda, I'm going to lunch. I can't take that smell any longer."

"I know what you mean."

Fifteen minutes later the woman came to the door, a hanky to her nose. "How much longer will you be?"

"Not over a half hour," Carter said, smiling.

"Well, hurry, will you?" She slammed the door behind her.

Carter went to work at once on the telephone. In seconds he had it apart. The relay transmitter was no bigger than the modem. There was more than enough room for the two of them to sit side by side when the case was replaced. The hookup was done easily with two tiny alligator clips. The wire leading under the desk to a booster unit about the size of a package of cigarettes wouldn't be discovered unless the whole unit—keyboard, computer, and telephone setup—were moved to the other side of the desk.

"All finished," Carter announced.

"Thank God."

He tucked the small receiver behind cleaning materials on the very top shelf of the eighth-floor maintenance closet. From that distance, reception would be perfect.

Shunning the elevators, he took the stairs to the basement. He unlocked two windows and the package-loading chute door from the inside, and stepped into the alley.

Ten minutes later he was headed north on the new highway toward Pretoria.

Several car lengths behind Carter, Bruno Copek sighed with relief. There were few exits on the expressway between J'burg and the forty-eight miles to Pretoria, and it was almost flat.

He could drop far behind and follow without worrying about detection as he had been forced to do all morning.

Pretoria was more than three hundred miles of streets with jacaranda trees. When they were in bloom, the whole city seemed purple.

Carter found Struban Street and checked into the Boulevard Hotel. In his room he dropped his bag and went for the phone.

"Baals Investments."

"This is Carter, Inez. Should I come to the office?"

"Herr Baals doesn't think it's wise."

"What then?"

"There's an Irish pub on Cabon Mare Street near Buyers Park. It's called Murphy's. I can meet you there around three."

"Fine," Carter said. "Do you still have your lines open?"

"It's still working hours," she replied.

"I've got a name, Jacob Preeva, and an address, just a box number, really: Alkfhor One-eleven."

"I think that's a village higher in the Transvaal. I can check. What do you need to know?"

"Family history, as much as possible, and a little more explicit address."

"See you at three."

The pub sat on a corner, and it seemed to be the "must stop" for tourists to pose for snapshots. It was all wood with tables and booths rising in tiers from a round bar in the center.

Carter arrived a little early and sat with his hands folded over a stein of beer. Occasionally, as he cased the crowd, he drank. Since entering the pub, he had acquired an itch. He sensed that someone was watching him with more than an occasional or idle interest.

Then he spotted him . . . big, broad shoulders with tanned leather for a face and cool steady eyes. Carter returned the man's stare, then the other looked away as if in embarrassment.

Inez entered, looked quickly around, and moved to the table. "Sorry I'm a bit late."

"I was a bit early. Beer?"

"Please."

Carter held up two fingers and the steins appeared as if by magic. The Killmaster raised his to his lips and talked around the rim. "To your right, about six tables back, tall, tanned, white jacket."

Her eyes swiveled around, then darted back to Carter's. "My husband," she said with a smile. "I told him I was meeting you here. We're having dinner and going to a show after."

Carter sighed with relief and threw the man a smile that was returned. "What have you got?"

"Nothing new from Mrs. Braxton. On Hans Veerdelph's old girl friend?"

"Yes?"

"She's a hairdresser, not too bright, and for the last year or so she's only worked now and then. But in that year she's amassed quite a sizable bank account."

"How sizable?" Carter asked.

"About seventy thousand pounds."

Carter whistled. "It had to come from Veerdelph," he said.

"She's also made several trips out of the country, about every two months."

"Where?"

"From the airline records, all the tickets were to Tunis. It's impossible to say if that was her last destination. Here's her number and address."

Carter glanced at it. "Here in Pretoria. Good. What about Jacob Preeva?"

An envelope came across the table. "Family tree, personal background, and current whereabouts. It's pretty complete. Also, we were able to identify that composite picture."

"Who?" Carter asked.

"The head of Aadlon. Christopher Boulda."

FOURTEEN

There are few seedy areas of Pretoria. If you were white, you were rich, or at least middle class. Crolla Snyder lived in a less than affluent area. The building was called the Sunvaal, and she lived in 3C.

He rang the bell, then knocked, then called her name. With no reply after a minute, he went to work on the locks with his picks.

He pushed the door shut behind him and looked around the apartment. An empty hall, an empty drawing room, an empty dining room, all furnished in expensive bad taste.

Carter moved into the bedroom. Its owner was obviously a devotee of American movie stars and bad local art. This was evidenced by the posters and paintings on the wall. From the closet he surmised that Mrs. Snyder had a preference for the leatherette punk look.

He disabled the telephone, wanting no interruptions when Crolla Snyder got home. His hand was halfway to his pocket for a cigarette when he noticed a lack of ashtrays in the apartment.

Two seconds inside and a nonsmoker would know

the place had been "violated." He killed the desire for a cigarette and got a Crown lager out of the refrigerator instead.

It was nearly an hour before he heard footsteps on the stairs, voices, and a key in the door.

"Damn," he hissed to himself, realizing that the woman wasn't alone.

He moved from the couch to a closet and stepped inside, leaving the door open a crack.

The outer door slammed and Carter heard a woman giggle. "God, Tommy, can't you wait until after dinner?"

"Sure I can, luv. But why bother?"

It was a man's voice. Then he came into Carter's line of sight. He was short, with a pasty face, longish but neat black hair, and a thin mustache. In some parts of the world he might be considered dapper. Carter thought he looked like a pimp.

Crolla Snyder was about what the Killmaster had expected . . . big, busty, and blond, with an inch of mascara and a short dress a size and a half too small in the hips and bust.

He watched them move to the middle of the room. Tommy had his arms wrapped around the woman from behind, his hands working the front of her dress, his face in her neck, and his groin rubbing against her buttocks.

Carter heard another giggle and the sound of a zipper, and groaned to himself.

If he waited now it was liable to take forever.

He eased the closet door open and stepped into the room. He coughed and, at the same time, slammed the closet door.

Tommy strangled a scream and almost jumped out of

his skin getting away from the woman. "Bitch," he croaked, "I thought you said you had no husband!"

Carter stepped forward and Tommy threw his hands up protectively in front of his face. Crolla Snyder stood glued to the floor, her mouth hanging open and her breasts hanging out where the partially unzipped dress gaped open.

Suddenly she found her voice. "I never saw him before!"

Carter pointed at Tommy. "You, sit down over there and shut up. I want to talk to the lady."

Tommy caught it and instantly recovered his poise. Now he was angry at Carter for making him look like a coward in front of the woman.

"Who the hell are you? You a burglar, some goddamned thief? I'm calling the police!"

"No," Carter said, his voice barely a whisper. "You just go play with yourself for a few minutes and everything will be fine. I need to talk to the lady."

"Who the hell do you think you are . . ."

Tommy lunged for the telephone. Carter glided forward two quick steps and glanced an open-handed right off the man's jaw.

"Sit down."

"Fuck you!"

Tommy swung a weak right. Carter stepped aside and popped him solidly in the gut with a short left, high, up under the breastbone. He caught the other man and laid him out unconscious on the couch.

He turned and faced Crolla. "In there," he growled, jerking his chin toward the kitchen.

He followed her and got two beers from the fridge, opened them, and put them on the table. "Sit down," he said, and took a chair facing her.

"Who are you?" she whimpered.

"Who gave you the money, Crolla?"

"What?"

"Crolla, listen very carefully." Carter abruptly shifted to Dutch, speaking fluently and fast. "Girl, fix yourself on this. I came for information. I won't leave without it. You saw what one punch did to your boyfriend. The fact that you're a woman means nothing to me. Understand?"

She stared at him for a moment, then sighed and nodded wearily. "I understand."

"Good." Carter sipped his beer. "In the past couple of years, you've worked one, maybe two days a week as a hairdresser. I know you're not selling your ass, so how did you get seventy thousand in the bank?"

She blinked but didn't hesitate. "An old boyfriend. I'm keeping it for him."

"What's his name?"

"Hans Veerdelph."

"Did you know Hans bought it a few days ago?"

"What?"

"Veerdelph is dead."

She smiled and her eyes lit up like pound signs.

"That's right, Crolla, he's dead. The money is all yours."

"Poor Hans," she said, the smile still on her face.

"Yeah, poor bastard." Carter took a swallow of beer and with a gesture indicated that she do the same. He gulped the last of the bottle and set it on the table. "Who did he work for?"

"I don't know," she said with a shrug. It was a cocky shrug.

Carter's hand flashed out and seized her throat. He clamped hard for an instant and watched as utter panic bulged in the woman's eyes. When she started to gag he released her.

"I ask questions, you answer. Got that?"

Crolla nodded, swallowing thickly. "My throat . . ."

"You're alive. Who did Veerdelph work for?"

"I only know a name," she croaked. "I heard Hans speak to him on the phone, called him Herr Boulda."

"Now you're cooking, Crolla. According to his passport, Veerdelph hasn't been in South Africa for six years—"

She interrupted with a laugh. "Up until a year ago he was here every month or so, even though the police wanted him for questioning about something. He bragged about it, said the real people in the government were on his side." She paused. "Do I really get to keep the money?"

Carter felt bile rise in his throat but he suppressed it. "Yeah, Crolla, it's all yours. You visited him several times. You flew to Tunis. Is that where you saw him?"

She shook her head. "I always flew to Tunis, but there I would take another flight."

"To where?"

"It varied. Sometimes Paris, Rome, all over."

"But where did you eventually meet up with Veerdelph?"

"Athens, always Athens. He'd meet me at the airport in this big Mercedes and we'd drive to his villa."

"His villa?" Carter said. "In Greece?"

"*Ja*. It was near a place called Vólos. It was big, real posh, and right on the sea. It even had its own little yacht harbor."

"And Veerdelph owned it?"

She smiled. "I know what you're thinking, and I thought the same thing. How the hell could a sometime mercenary own a Greek villa? But he did. He even showed me the deed. It was paid for."

Vólos, Carter thought. They hadn't even taken Joanna Lloyd out of the country.

He stood and dropped an American ten on the table. "That's for the beers, Crolla. Buy one for your boyfriend when he wakes up."

Her smile was ear to ear. "You think I'm going to fool with that little creep now that I'm a rich woman?"

Carter turned his back and left the apartment.

One more stop, he thought, driving back to the hotel. First thing in the morning he would drive up into the high Transvaal and see Jacob Preeva.

By the time he left Preeva he was pretty sure he would have the whole thing.

It was four in the morning, the dead hour, when a normal man's reactions were slowest and his sleep was the deepest.

But Carter hadn't survived for years in the killing business by being a normal man.

The instant the rhythm of sound changed, his eyes popped open and his body tensed.

What was it? A click, and then a slight scrape.

Without moving a muscle, he rolled his eyes to the open glass doors leading to the small balcony. Suddenly a hulk blotted out the moon and Carter moved. He rolled to the floor and then kept rolling toward the hulk.

The click he had heard was the safety of a gun being released. The two dull pops, like champagne corks being softly released from a bottle, were unmistakable. He didn't have to look to know that right now two slugs were embedded in the mattress where, two seconds before, he had been sleeping.

Three feet from the man, Carter came up in a crouch, grabbed the man's right forearm, and slammed the wrist against the doorframe.

There was a grunt of pain and the heavy automatic hit the carpet. At the same time, Carter swung under the arm and twisted it.

His intent was to drive the man down to the floor face-first. It didn't work that way. The hulk was bigger than Carter had first estimated, much bigger, and faster.

With a growl he came out of Carter's grasp and whirled. The Killmaster had no choice. He went on the offensive, dipping and driving his shoulder into the man's groin. He wrapped his hands behind the other man's knees and locked his left wrist in his right hand.

For the second time the surprise was momentarily Carter's. He drove forward, jerking his chin up, tightening his neck and stomach muscles.

But the big man recovered with very fast instincts. The moment Carter hit him, he began clubbing the Killmaster's head with one fist and pummeling his kidneys with the other.

They hit the far wall with a crashing thud and Carter jerked free. He slid to the side, fast, but the hulk moved with incredible swiftness. Carter had a fraction of a second to jerk back and roll his face away so the kick caught him along the neck and under the chin instead of full in the face.

Carter looped his right arm out and caught the man's leg, clutched a handful of cloth, jumped up and into him, holding on and pulling higher. The big man danced for balance on one foot, then swayed aside, and as he began falling, Carter shoved the leg higher and the man fell. As he dropped, Carter slid his hands down the leg and gripped the man's foot in both hands, twisting.

The man grunted as Carter twisted and lashed with his free foot. It felt like a mule's kick on Carter's thigh. He stepped astride the man's leg, twisting with all his power, and doubled the knee, forcing it back upon itself. The man cried out in pain. Carter kept the pressure on, knowing the cry a fake, and the man kicked him again with his free foot.

Carter shot back his right leg as hard as he could and felt the softness give as his heel drove into the man's crotch. This time the agonizing cry was real.

Carter kicked again, once more, felt the foot and ankle in his hands go limp. He dropped the foot and sprang away.

He flipped on the lights and found the silenced automatic, a Mauser 7.63. The gun was a good thirty years old, but it looked new, cared for.

This one, Carter thought, was a pro.

Accompanied by the groans and gasps of the man on the floor, Carter pulled on a pair of pants.

"Roll over, asshole!"

He didn't move. He just lay blubbering and gripping his crotch. Carter drop-kicked him in the side and he went over on his belly, adding new curses to the grunts and groans.

From the small of the man's back Carter took a .380 Llama automatic. He found an eight-inch switchblade pigsticker on his right ankle, and an over-and-under Derringer in a Legster holster on his left ankle.

"You're a regular arsenal, aren't you, asshole!"

With one swift yank, the hulk's coat came down to his forearms, stifling any sudden moves. Deftly, the Killmaster's experienced hands went through the pockets. He removed a flat, thin wallet from the inside jacket pocket, and odds and ends including a set of car keys from the trouser pockets.

"Bruno Copek, from Capetown," Carter read from the driver's license. "Okay, Bruno, what's your story?"

Copek started to roll over. Carter cocked the Mauser

and ground the barrel of the silencer into the bone behind the man's left ear.

"No need to move, my man, you're perfect just where you are. Damn, you're a big one, aren't you? I imagine you'd dress out about two-seventy, two-eighty, wouldn't you?"

"Uncock the Mauser," the man growled. "That pin's been filed."

"No shit?" Carter murmured. "Then you'd better start talking before I breathe on it."

No good. The man had guts. Either he was sure Carter wouldn't kill him, or he just didn't care. The Killmaster decided on a new tactic, direct confrontation.

"On second thought, Bruno, roll over."

Taking care, as though he were lying on eggs, Copek rolled over. Grinning like a shark, Carter pointed the Llama right between his eyes.

"Who hired you to off me, Bruno?"

The big man was trembling but he never made a sound.

"I hope you're not Catholic, Bruno. There's no time for a priest."

Carter pulled the trigger.

The gun, of course, was empty. He had released the magazine and ejected the chambered shell the moment he found the gun.

Copek grinned. It was more like an evil leer. "The Mauser's silenced; the Llama isn't. I knew you wouldn't shoot me with the Llama and make a lot of noise."

"Smart boy, very smart boy," Carter said, "and tough. Get up, Bruno!"

For a moment, the wildness came back into the man's eyes. But Carter saw him fight himself for self-control, move, gathering himself. And then he came up fast at Carter, not believing Carter would shoot and have the noise pull the police down on them. He came low and fast.

Carter anticipated the move and shot his left heel up with a kick that would have downed a door. The blow caught Copek full on the upper lip and nose. He went all rubbery and sighed as he fell.

Carter moved to the bed and ripped the pillowcase into strips. He tied Copek's hands behind his back, tied his feet together, pulled the feet up, and tied them to the hands with a loop around Copek's neck.

He gripped him under the arms and dragged him into the bathroom. Leaving him crumpled on the cold tile floor, he flipped the stopper lever and turned on the water full force. The tub quickly began filling. Carter rolled the huge body over into the sunken tub, switched the lever to shower, and let the icy-cold needles wash across the side of Copek's face and chest.

The big man moaned, moving his head as though testing himself for a broken neck. His eyes fluttered open, the wildness exposed again.

Carter sat on the toilet lid and let the cold water drive all the haze and cobwebs from Copek's mind, and after a few minutes he snapped the water off.

"All right, asshole, let's talk."

Copek shook his head, his tongue probing the gaps where teeth had been. "What you want?"

"Look at it this way, Bruno. Getting shot is one thing. Drowning is another. It's a shitty way to die, Bruno. Your mind screams while your lungs fill up with water. It's a slow death, Bruno. Gimme a whistle if you change your mind." Carter rose from the commode, turned the tap back on to a steady stream, and moved to the door.

"No, damn you, no! What kind of man are you!" the giant sputtered.

"Same as you, Bruno, a heartless son of a bitch."

Carter left the bathroom with the water running in the tub. With the bottle from his bag he built himself a drink. Then he dressed and packed.

He guessed the timing about right and returned to the bathroom. The tub had filled enough so Copek survived only by thrusting himself up with all his strength, snuffling a gasp of air through his broken nose, falling back, then humping up again.

Carter walked over and looked down at him. He let Copek have a good look, then he raised his foot and shoved the man's head under the water and held it there. Copek's huge muscles bulged, veins standing out as he tried breaking the bonds, and then, after one final effort, his body went slack and a gush of pink bubbles flooded up from his nose.

Carter removed his foot. He got a towel, looped it under Copek's head around the side of his neck, and pulled him up out of the water. He pulled the stopper and let water drain from the tub. When it lowered enough, he let Copek fall back and watched the huge chest heave massively as he fought for air.

"Can you hear me, Bruno? Understand me?"

The big man grunted and managed to gasp, "Yeah."

"Good. I don't really need or want to kill you, big man. I just want to know who wants me out. Tell me that and you go. Promise."

The Killmaster watched as the man's thick brain digested and weighed his words. He was helped along a little when Carter reached to replace the stopper in the tub.

"Okay, okay. His name is Carl."

"Carl who?"

"I dunno, just Carl. He's a broker. I've worked maybe ten, twelve hits for him. He's got a whole stable.

Little guy, about five feet tall, sharp nose, black hair, got a Brit accent."

"He's in Capetown?"

"No, I think he works out of J'burg."

"How does it go down after I'm history?" Carter asked.

"I got a phone number. I call him, tell him the hit's made."

Carter fingered the Mauser. That was probably so Carl could inform the client. He dragged Bruno out of the tub and rolled him into the bedroom. He untied his wrists and retied them in front of him. Then he stuck the phone in his hands and the Mauser in his ear.

"You get any ideas of bashing me with the phone, Bruno, you still get one in the brain. What's the number?"

Copek told him and Carter dialed.

"Sound convincing, Bruno, very convincing," he hissed.

The number rang five times before a thin, sleep-drugged voice answered. "Yes?"

"Carl, me, Bruno."

"So?"

"So it's done."

"Where?"

"Hotel, Pretoria. In his bed."

"Good, Bruno, very good. Get out of the country for a while. Give me a call in a couple of months." The phone went dead.

Copek was sweating gallons when Carter took the receiver from his hands and hung it up.

"What now?"

"Where's your car parked?"

"Two blocks, across the park," Copek replied.

"Grab my bag. Let's go."

"With my hands tied?"

"Hold it in front of you, you're a strong boy."

They took the service stairs down to the garage and Carter's car. As he drove out of the garage he saw that the parking attendant's cubicle was dark and locked. The day man wouldn't come on until six. He had just about an hour.

Copek had done him a favor. The man's car was parked in a spot where the closest streetlight was two blocks away.

"Out," Carter growled, "around to the trunk of your car."

Copek did as he was told. Inside the trunk, Carter discovered the suitcase and the two aluminum cases inside it. He opened them, and whistled.

"Loaded for bear, weren't you, sport? Get in the trunk!"

"W-What you doing?"

"Nothing, yet," Carter said. "But you are. Get in the trunk."

Reluctantly, the man rolled his bulky body into the trunk. Carter retied his ankles and again attached them to his wrists. Then he stuck the Mauser into Copek's mouth.

"How many hits have you made in your life, sport?"

"What the hell . . . ?"

"How many?" Carter raked the end of the silencer along the roof of Copek's mouth.

"Forty-two."

"That's a long career for anybody," Carter said.

"Man, you promised!"

"I lied."

Carter put two slugs into his brain.

He wiped the guns clean and dropped them into the trunk beside Copek's body. He slammed the trunk, took the key from the ring, and threw it into the bushes. When the two aluminum cases were in the trunk of his own car, he drove Copek's car back to the hotel's underground parking lot and left it in a secluded corner.

He picked the lock on the door of the parking attendant's cubicle and punched out a long-term ticket on the machine. With the ticket underneath the windshield wiper of Copek's car, he walked back across the park to his own car.

Figuring a quick stop for breakfast, he should find Jacob Preeva by midmorning.

FIFTEEN

Once off the main road, the going was rough. Inez, in her directions, hadn't told him that without a four-wheel-drive vehicle he might not make it. But she probably hadn't known.

Gingerly he eased the car across the road's pock-marked surface and bounced along for a couple of miles in second gear. At last he rounded a curve, and before him he could see a sheet of water and rolling green hills dotted with the puff-ball shapes of sheep. He drew to a halt and rolled down the window, absorbing the scene.

"I think this is it," he said aloud.

He moved on again, hurrying now, feeling the holes in the road menace his axle, until at last he reached a lake shore and a clump of trees. A mile beyond him was a hut, and from its chimney soft feathers of smoke drifted up in the still air.

Carter drove past the trees, then backed the car in behind them. If anything, the ground seemed easier than the road. He got out, walked to the road, and stared intently. The car was perfectly hidden. He took off all his weapons and left them in the car.

He struck out for the hut. He passed over two low, rolling hills and found himself among rows of vines. Beyond the vines was a neat kitchen garden with orderly lines of melons, pumpkins, and tomatoes, and beyond that the wall of the cottage and a closed door.

Just in front of the door a huge dog lolled, his massive head on his forepaws.

Carter called out, "Herr Preeva? Jacob Preeva!"

As the door started to open, the dog stood. Instantly he changed from big and cuddly to something like a wolf, teeth bared, mouth opened to snarl.

A man's voice quieted him. The man stayed in the shadows beyond the door. When the dog sat down, the man shouted at Carter.

"I don't speak Afrikaans, Herr Preeva," Carter interrupted. "Dutch . . . German . . . English?"

"I speak English. What do you want? Who are you?"

"My name is Carter. I am with the Capetown office of Amalgamated Press and Wire Services. I'm a journalist."

"Newspaperman?"

"Yes, in a way."

"I don't read newspapers. Go away."

"Herr Preeva, please, I'm trying to do a series of articles on old families in South Africa. You could help me very much."

"No."

"Herr Preeva, I've talked to your daughters. I'd like to talk to you."

The man stepped into the yard carrying a shotgun crooked in one arm. He was a white-bearded, florid-faced man in a T-shirt and worn coveralls. His body was lean, aged, with yellowish skin and thin, weak-looking arms.

Carter took a chance and approached until he was only a few feet from the man.

"My daughters don't have anything to do with me. They think I'm crazy."

Carter smiled. "I'd like to find out for myself."

Preeva stared at Carter for a full minute. "You drink?"

"I'd love a drink."

"Come inside."

The Preeva family history went back to the Boar War and before. Jacob Preeva was the last male in the line. As far as he was concerned, he was the *only* Preeva.

He had married in his forties, an English girl he met in London. There were two daughters, Hulda and Jane. His wife died just after the youngest daughter, Jane, was born.

"Tried to raise 'em myself, raise 'em to be ladies. Didn't like this life, though. Wanted the city life, money, fine clothes."

"And do you know where are they now, Herr Preeva?"

"As soon as they were old enough they ran off, started whoring. I disowned 'em, I did."

"But they send you money every month?"

He nodded and growled. "Conscience money. The older girl Hulda, she likes other girls. Filthy business."

"And the younger one, Jane?"

"Married some crook, a con man from Amsterdam."

"Christopher Boulda."

"That's him. He's a jailbird. Supposed to be some kind of engineer. Heard he embezzled money. Got caught."

"And is he still married to Jane?"

"No, she died about three years ago. Hulda sent me a

letter, told me about it. Didn't go to the funeral, didn't want to."

"Herr Preeva, I have some pictures. This one . . ."

Carefully, Carter set one of the two photographs he had taken from Hulda's scrapbook in front of the old man.

A pair of wire-rimmed spectacles came from a pocket of the faded coveralls. Preeva carefully adjusted them to his ears and stared intently at the picture. When he spoke it was in a husky whisper.

"That's when we were a family, a happy family."

"I can see that," Carter said, not pushing.

"That's me there with Hulda on my knee. That's my wife holding the baby."

"Jane?"

"*Ja,*" he said, nodding.

"And this photo, Herr Preeva?" Carter set the second picture on the table. It was a shot of Hulda and Jane with a tall, raw-boned woman with long blond hair. "This picture would have been taken about two years later. Jane was a toddler then."

Again the old man nodded. Now there were tears in his eyes behind the thick glasses. "*Ja.* That was when my wife died, just after."

"Who is the woman in the picture, Herr Preeva?"

"My wife's sister, from England. She came out here after my wife died to help with the children for a while."

"Then she was Jane and Hulda's aunt?"

"*Ja.* She had just lost her husband in an auto accident."

"And the third child, the one in her arms?"

"Her baby. She was about a year younger than Jane."

"What was your sister-in-law's name, Herr Preeva?"

"Frawley, Gertrude Frawley."

Carter nodded. "She was from Cornwall, wasn't she?"

"*Ja, ja,* Cornwall."

"A place called Trevone Bay?"

The old man removed his glasses. He wiped his eyes and stared intently at Carter. "You ask a lot of questions."

"I'm a journalist."

"Are you?"

Carter weighed it before he spoke. "Yes, I am ... among other things."

The old man got stiffly to his feet and moved to a sideboard. He took out a small box and returned to the table. The box seemed to be full of photos and old, yellowing letters.

"*Ja, ja,* here it is, Trevone Bay. Gertrude stayed with us for almost two years, helping me with the children. Then she went back to England, to Trevone Bay in Cornwall. She wrote for a few years and then I never heard from her again."

"Herr Preeva, what happened to Gertrude's child?"

The old man stood and walked to a window in the rear of the cottage, motioning Carter to follow him.

"She's there."

Carter followed the old man's pointed finger to a small enclosure atop a nearby hill. He could make out two stones beside two well-tended graves.

"She was a sickly child. She died about a year after Gertrude came. We laid her to rest up there, beside my wife."

Carter sighed. "Thanks for all your help, Herr Preeva." He gathered the photographs from the table and headed for the door.

"Carter..."

He turned. The old man was still staring out the window.

"Yes?"

"My girl, Hulda. She's in trouble, isn't she."

"I'm afraid so, Herr Preeva. A lot of trouble."

The skinny shoulders sagged and the gray head fell forward. "I think I always knew she would be."

Carter left the cottage and climbed the hill. The stone was caked with dust, and he had to brush it with his hand in order to read the crudely chiseled inscriptions:

B. 1963—D. 1965

JOANNA FRAWLEY

R.I.P.

SIXTEEN

He made one stop, a small hotel to call Inez and pick up a newspaper.

"His name is Carl. That's all I have, besides the number, 34-9611. I'll call you from Johannesburg when I get in."

Inez gave him her apartment number in Pretoria.

Over a sandwich and a cup of coffee, he scoured the newspaper. There was no story about a body in the trunk of the car parked in a hotel parking garage in Pretoria.

It was dark and it had started to rain by the time he hit downtown Johannesburg. He drove directly to the building housing the offices of Aadlon International.

The door to the package chute was locked from the inside. So was one of the windows. The other, several feet from the floor on the inside, wasn't.

Silently, Carter dropped into the basement and made his way up the stairs to the eighth floor. The recorder was exactly where he had left it, and three quarters of the spool had gone through.

Back on the street he placed a long-distance call, collect, to Bud Corliss's private number in Athens.

"God, am I glad to hear from you!"

"How did the runaround go?" Carter asked.

"Just that, a runaround. The senator took the first phone call in Mrs. Braxton's attorney's office. We had the car waiting outside just like they said."

"And?"

"They ran him all over Athens and halfway up to Thebes, outdoor pay phones, hotel lobbies, restaurants. It went on for hours."

"And no demands," Carter said.

"None. At the last stop he was told to go back to the yacht. Next contact, forty-eight hours."

"It's a stall," Carter growled.

"Yeah, but what for? If they're not going to make a ransom demand, why snatch her?"

"Time," Carter said. "I'll tell you about it when I get back. Did MI5 come up with anything new on Joanna Lloyd?"

"A few things. The initial clearance investigation by our people was pretty spotty . . . senator's wife, I guess."

"Like what?"

"School records, for one. They are intact and still there, but no one at the schools seems to remember her. Also, the mother, Gertrude Frawley . . ."

"What about her?" Carter asked.

"Mrs. Lloyd listed her as dead."

Carter smiled. "And she's not."

"No. She's in a mental hospital in Truro, England. Nice place. Mrs. Lloyd has been paying the bills. The senator shrugged it off, said it's probably because she was embarrassed."

"A lot more than that," Carter murmured. "Get back with London. Have them go back to the hospital, interview nurses, doctors, orderljes, everyone who has been there for a while."

"What are we looking for?" Corliss asked.

"Who visited her, when, what took place when they did. There has to be some kind of a record. Also, check out Christopher Boulda in Amsterdam. He's a con man and an embezzler. He's also done some time."

"Will do. That it?"

"I'm taking the eleven-forty out of here for Rome—"

"Rome?"

Carter laughed. "Yeah, I'm supposed to be dead, so it won't look good if I show up at the Athens airport. Tell Chandra to have the helicopter pick me up in Rome."

He killed the connection and waited until the operator came back on the line. He gave her the Pretoria number, and Inez picked up on the first ring.

"Hello?"

"Me," Carter said.

She didn't waste time with words that weren't needed. "That phone number you gave me is listed to an escort service, Merrytime. It rings through to another number in the Grofe section of Johannesburg, One-fourteen Delph Avenue. The address lists out as owned by one Miranda Dopez."

"Little Carl doesn't take any chances, does he?" Carter said.

"There's no mention of any Carl. Are you sure you've got the right number?"

"Good question, but I've got a description. That's all I'll need."

"Are you off soon?"

"I hope so. I want you to book me on the eleven-forty to Rome. Use the alias on the papers you gave me. Tell them it's a special handling case."

"What kind of special handling?" she asked.

"A recovering burn victim. Can you get a lot of bandages, a good-sized robe, two white coats—ones that will fit you and your husband—and the use of an ambulance?"

Inez sighed. "Somehow."

"Good. I'll meet you in that little restaurant outside the airport."

"Rudolph's?"

"You got it. Eleven sharp."

There was a single light on in the upstairs bedroom of Aadlon's chief accountant, Nils Zefsheem.

Carter made a complete turn around the block, then parked several blocks away.

When the Killmaster came in through a window at the rear of the house, he could hear a television going strong in the upstairs bedroom.

He had cut the wires of a rudimentary alarm system before entering, so he got in quietly. He came into the thickly carpeted corridor with its potted palms and paintings, and saw the darkened sitting room door. He glanced in, then moved on down the hall to the study. He entered the room silently, on cat feet.

The antique clock in a corner ticked audibly. Somewhere outside, a dog barked. Carter went directly to the painting and stood before it for a moment, then reached behind its right-hand edge. There was a small clicking sound, and the painting swung outward on hinges, revealing the wall safe.

He stood, inspecting it. It was a double combination, a bit complex but manageable.

He rubbed his fingertips on the rough stone wall around the edge of the safe, and then began turning the first dial. It took him only a few minutes of listening to indistinct clicking noises to unlock the first lock. The second one gave him more trouble, but finally it, too, yielded to his expert touch. A moment later he swung the safe door open, and there was no alarm.

He pursed his lips in a silent whistle as he gazed at the safe. It was most unusual. Normal safes are the same diameter as the door containing the dial face and some eighteen inches or two feet deep. This box was a *real* safe, steel-lined, cemented in place. Inside, it measured three feet deep and two feet wide.

He stripped an embroidered case from one of the couch pillows and packed the money first, by rough count about two hundred thousand English pounds. All of it was in low-denomination, well-used bills, all banded in packets with totals on the bands.

Carter guessed this was running money for Zefsheem and his boyfriend if anything blew up in their faces.

There were three large ledgers. Carter had only to run his penlight over a few pages of each one of them to realize that he had struck gold.

Evidently, Herr Zefsheem and Herr Boulda went back a long way. Aadlon was only the latest in a long line of scams, from Tokyo to Paris to Johannesburg.

Like the money, Carter thought, these ledgers were probably part of Zefsheem's insurance policy, in case Boulda ever got it into his head to screw his bookkeeper.

The rest of the safe's contents were jewelry, a coin collection, some gold, and personal papers. Carter left it.

He put the ledgers in with the money, then took a letter opener from the desk and jammed the tumblers inside the safe. To get it open again would take an expert with a drill. It might even have to be blown. All that would take at least a couple of days. Even then, with the money gone they might think it was just a burglar who had overlooked the smaller stuff.

Carter closed and locked the safe and, silently as a stalking lion, left the way he had entered.

The Delph section of Johannesburg was on the burgeoning north side. It was an area of new, substantial ranch-style homes plopped in the middle of one- and two-acre tracts. All the homes looked comfortable but not ostentatious.

Obviously Carl didn't flash his wealth.

One-fourteen Delph Avenue was at the end of a cul-de-sac, with the homes on either side a good distance away because of the lot size. There was a two-door garage attached to the side of the house, with a large, roll-up door in front and a small door to the side.

Carter swung very slowly around the cul-de-sac, letting his lights play through the windows of the large garage door.

Two cars. A little Ford Cortina and a very large Rover sedan. It didn't take a genius to figure out which one would be Carl's.

But he had to make sure. He drove back to the head of the cul-de-sac and then around the corner. He killed his lights and then stopped by shifting into neutral and using the hand brake. Using the butt of his Luger, he smashed the dome light and left the car.

He skirted an empty field and came up behind 114. He made noise at first so he would alert any dogs. When he was greeted by no barks or beasts, he vaulted the rear wall and approached the rear patio.

The drapes were pulled open from a large picture window in the bedroom. Inside, a woman was sitting up in bed, the covers crossing her lap but not entirely concealing her lower body. Her skin was olive-toned, giving her a Latin look. Her hair was black, which contributed to the same impression. It was sexily tangled—half up and half twisted around. She had dark eyes, a prominent nose, and a lush mouth from which her vivid lipstick had been partially chewed off. But her breasts were by far her most attractive features. Carter looked at them —heavy and full and abundantly round, with large nipples that resembled ripe cherries.

If he'd had any doubts about this being Miranda Dopez, they were quieted when Carl, in dark trousers and a smoking jacket, entered the room. Bruno Copek had described him exactly.

A big woman like Miranda Dopez would fit Carl's type, if he could afford her. Carter was sure he could.

Carter retraced his steps to the car.

In the back seat, working by feel and the faint moonlight that filtered through the windows, he opened the two cases. One appeared empty, with a thick, jellylike lining. From the other case he took a sharp knife. He sliced a straight line across the bottom lining. The blade sank in three inches. He made a parallel cut, then one across each end. Carefully he lifted out a strip of plastique twenty inches long and four inches wide.

From the foam rubber underside of the lid he removed a long flat box. He opened it, and inside lay a variety of mercury fulminate detonators—blasting caps wrapped in cotton on foam rubber padding. The case had been made especially for these. The deadly caps were so extremely sensitive that sudden changes in atmospheric pressure or temperature, or shock, could detonate them.

Bruno Copek knew his business.

The last items Carter removed from the case were a pair of alligator clips and a three-foot length of wire.

This time he strolled right down the sidewalk in front

of the houses. Just past 114, he darted up the grass median by the drive and crouched by the side door.

It was unlocked.

At the Cortina, he lifted the hood and removed the distributor rotor. With the hood of the Cortina back down, secured and wiped clean of prints, he moved over to the Rover.

Working by feel alone, it took Carter less than ninety seconds to plant the charge, molding the plastique around the steering column tightly, inserting the electric detonator and wiring it to the nearest spark plug. He lowered the hood, slipped the latch, pushed the hood down, released the latch, and locked the hood in place.

He faded through the shadows back across the street and waited five minutes. He'd awakened no one. He moved out, light-footed, quick, along the fronts of the houses to the end of the block, then crossed the street and walked back to his car, got in and drove away.

The turn onto the airport expressway was about two miles from 114 Delph Avenue. There was an all-night gas station with a pay phone at the edge of the access road.

Carter parked in the shadows near the station and walked back out to the end of the road.

The call went through exactly like the one Copek had made at the hotel. It rang five times and then there was a series of clicks as Merrytimes' interim phone sent the call on to the woman's house.

"Hello?" It was the woman.

"Let me speak to Carl."

"Jus'a minute."

There was the sound of a hushed conversation, and then the voice Carter remembered—high, a little tense —came on the line. "Yes, this is Carl. What is it?"

"Listen up, Carl, and listen up good. This is Carter, Nick Carter..."

"Wha—"

"Shut up and listen, Carl. Your boy Bruno blew it. I'm at the airport. And do you know what I'm doing, Carl? I'm looking at a map of J'burg. There's a circle on the map around one-fourteen Delph Avenue. I'm coming for you, scum. Tell Miranda, your big-busted girl friend, to stick around. She can watch you get castrated."

Carter hung up and walked into the service station. He bought one orange Fanta and a candy bar and returned to the car.

For three minutes he leaned against the hood of the car, drank his soda, munched his candy bar, and stared at the night sky.

From two miles away the big boom, when it came, was more like the aftermath of a plane passing through the sound barrier, a rolling thud.

But it was the orange ball rising into the night sky that told the real tale.

"Can you breathe?" Inez asked.

"Yeah," Carter mumbled through the bandages covering his face and head. "But it's hotter than hell, though."

"The wheelchair's collapsible, so you can use it in Rome," she said.

Her husband came around the side of the ambulance and opened the rear doors. "Ready?"

"Yeah," Carter said, stowing the ledgers in his bag. "Be careful how you dispose of those aluminum cases. One of them is lined with plastique. And dump the detonators in a pond somewhere. Water makes them useless."

Inez and her husband exchanged a quick look. It was obvious that they had both heard the big boom and all the sirens north of the city.

Carter went on, "Does Baals pay you pretty well for what you do?"

Inez smiled. "Pretty well. But I must say, I don't do much of this."

"You did fine," Carter said, and turned to the husband. "What do you do?"

"I'm a teacher."

Carter handed him the pillowcase containing the money.

"What's this?"

Carter lay down on the stretcher. Beneath the bandages, he grinned. "A donation to higher education," he said. "Let's go."

SEVENTEEN

Carter slept the whole flight from Johannesburg to Rome. Chandra had flown in on the chopper to pick him up. She had been contacted by Bud Corliss before her departure; he would join them on the *Noble Savage* as soon as he had confirmed all the information Carter had requested.

During the return flight to the *Noble Savage*, Chandra briefed Carter and he instructed her.

Senator Samuel Lloyd was in bad shape, for several reasons. He was ragged about his wife. Also, the tension of not knowing what the kidnappers wanted for her ransom made it worse for him to cope with the "not knowing" situation.

That morning, he had demanded that Chandra inform the authorities in Greece, Italy, and at Interpol. She had managed to sidestep him for the moment, but she didn't think she could stall him much longer.

To make matters worse, the senator had talked by phone to his aides in Washington and New York. Preliminary vote counts in the U.N. and in Congress for his plan for total Namibian independence predicted failure.

His people had urged him to return at once. If he didn't, they had assured him, the plan was doomed.

When it came Carter's turn, he gave Chandra a complete rundown on what had occurred in South Africa. Remembering her earlier queasiness, he left out mentioning the attempted hit on him, and the deaths of Bruno Copek and his broker, Carl.

He handed over the ledgers, the tape recording from the computer transactions in Aadlon's offices, and the telephone bill from Zefsheem's home, with instructions to get the latter to Bud Corliss as soon as possible.

Chandra told him she had two of her lawyers and an investments analyst waiting on the yacht to start sifting through the information the moment they set down.

"It doesn't look good, does it?" she sighed as the chopper circled the stern of the gleaming white yacht. "What will you do?"

"That depends on Senator Sam's reaction."

"If you can get a reaction other than anger from him," she replied. "I haven't."

The rotors were still spinning as they dived out of the cockpit. Clutching the tape and the ledgers, Chandra took off at a dead run for the bridge and the communications room. Carter headed for his cabin and a shower and shave. But first he stopped in the main salon where a steward informed him that the senator was inside, at the bar.

Sam Lloyd looked like hell. His eyes were red holes in an ashen face, and he sported a good two days' growth of beard. The once immaculate clothes were now a wrinkled mess, and there was a dark ring around the collar of his shirt.

He was slumped against the bar on his elbows, a bottle and glass in front of him.

"Carter..."

"Senator." The Killmaster moved around behind the bar and poured himself three fingers.

"What happened? Where do we stand?" The voice was an octave or so above normal, not quite hysteria but getting there. The words were also slurred.

"It was an eventful trip." Carter downed the drink and poured another.

"Goddamnit, Carter, is that any answer?" Now it was a shriek, and Carter saw the anger Chandra had mentioned.

"Calm down, Senator."

"The hell I will! I want some answers, results!"

"I think we'll have some for you soon."

"How soon?" Lloyd demanded.

"A few hours. Maybe less."

"They've probably killed Joanna already. That's why they don't want to negotiate."

"I doubt that," Carter said dryly.

Lloyd leaned over the bar, his red-rimmed eyes struggling to focus. "Carter, I don't like your attitude," he snarled. "Who is your superior in Washington?"

Carter met his gaze. "A very mean man. Tell me something, Senator . . ."

"What now?"

"Would you entertain a suggestion?"

"Such as?"

"This crucial vote on Namibia. It's only three days away now, right?"

"That's right."

"Chandra tells me it's not going too well."

The shoulders sagged even more. "It isn't. In fact, it's all but lost."

"Would it help if you were back there to sway a few people, in person?"

"Of course it would."

"Then I think you should go back, now, today."

Lloyd's face flushed red. He tried to rise but slumped back on the stool. "You're mad."

"Not really," Carter replied. "At this point I think you can do more good there than you can here."

"They have already said that they will talk only to me! I can't leave here, Carter. My God, it would jeopardize everything!"

"Then that's your last word?"

"Yes, definitely."

"Even though you've spent nearly five years of your career on this project?"

The voice and the face softened slightly. "Joanna is more important to me than politics."

Carter sighed and headed for the door, pausing to turn back to the man at the bar. "You know, Senator, I figured you would say that."

"What are you going to do?"

"Get a shower and a shave," Carter threw over his shoulder. "And I suggest you do the same. I can smell you almost as much as I can myself."

The communications room was a beehive of activity. Chandra and the computer ace, Ryder, were banging away. Their faces were grim, but the more they worked, the closer their lips came to smiling.

"How's it going?" Carter asked.

"Fine, sir," Ryder replied.

Chandra was more effusive. "All the access codes were on that tape. Jesus, Nick, we're breaking the bank! Another half hour and we'll have it all."

The Killmaster sipped his coffee and moved across to three men who sat conferring at the conference table. He introduced himself, and Amos Treadwell, a tall, aristocratic man in his sixties, returned the introductions.

"What have you got so far?" Carter asked.

"We're going over the ledgers, and then we run through the printouts of what they are bringing up on these Aadlon accounts." He nodded toward Ryder and Chandra. "Some of it is past history. A little of it seems to do with the Namibia project. All of it, I'm telling you, is fascinating."

"Anything yet?"

"Oh, yes, quite a bit, actually. And a great deal of it has been verified through Interpol and several international banks."

"From the ledgers?"

"Yes. This Boulda chap and Zefsheem make quite a team. I'm not an expert on criminal law, but I'd say there's enough here to put the two of them away for life plus a hundred years or so, at least. Probably this Preeva woman as well."

"How soon can you get me a complete breakdown and your recommendations?"

"Another two hours should do it, I'd say."

"Good enough," Carter said. "Thank you for coming over, Mr. Treadwell."

"Don't mention it. I was on the board of three of the companies these buggers swindled!"

Carter heard the chopper returning, and excused himself. He met Bud Corliss halfway up the ladder, turned him around, and led him to his cabin.

"Coffee?" the Killmaster asked.

"Please."

"What have you got?"

"A ton. There were over twenty calls from Zefsheem's phone in Johannesburg to a private number in

Vólos. The billing cycle on the receipt you got was through two days ago."

"Who owns the number?"

"Hans Veerdelph," Corliss replied. "At least the phone—like the villa in Vólos—is in his name."

"And Hans Veerdelph is dead, disappeared."

"But the number is still very active." Corliss was grinning from ear to ear. "And now on to the bills from the house in Crotone . . ."

"Ugo Belladini."

"Right. Five calls to a pay phone in a taverna outside Vólos. I checked. The taverna is about a mile down the road from the villa registered to Veerdelph."

Carter lit a cigarette, inhaled deeply, and exhaled with a relaxed sigh. "So that's where they are."

"Looks like it," Corliss said, nodding. "Now about this other. Your pal at MI5, Harley Donne, made another swing through Cornwall. Four people at the hospital remember an attorney dropping by to see Gertrude Frawley."

"About four years ago?" Carter asked.

"Right. It seems he was there twice a month for about six months. He had her sign a lot of papers, and then he just never came back. But the money for her care started coming in regularly."

"Description?" Carter said.

"Matches Nils Zefsheem to a T. He was a busy fellow. He also got around to a lot of schools. Donne seems to think some money passed hands to insert some records. He wants to know if he should follow it up."

Carter shook his head. "No need. I think we've got enough."

"Jesus, Nick, is that how they pulled it off?"

Carter nodded. "Gertrude Frawley's little girl died in the Transvaal. Back then, they barely had roads, and no neighbors. There was a birth certificate filed in England, but no death certificate. As long as Gertrude was kept quiet, Joanna Frawley was still alive."

"So when they put all this together, Jane Preeva-Boulda just became Joanna Frawley?"

"And then Joanna Lloyd," Carter said. "What were you able to get on Boulda?"

"Bad boy," Corliss replied. "He's been chased out of several countries, indicted a dozen times, but only convicted once. He did two years in Belgium for a stock swindle. He was Christopher Balsom then. He became Boulda when he hit South Africa. That reminds me. I checked with B.O.S.S. in Pretoria . . ."

"And there's a death certificate and a grave for Jane Boulda," Carter finished for him.

"Yeah."

"Where did she die?"

"Liberia. She was on a business trip with her husband."

Carter laughed. "In Liberia I could buy the national seal if I could pay for it. I imagine a death certificate would go for about fifty dollars."

"But who's in the grave in Johannesburg?"

"Some poor street girl, probably. Murder wouldn't bother Boulda when the stakes are this high."

"What tipped you to Joanna?" Corliss asked. "To the idea that it was a phony kidnapping?"

"She herself did, actually," Carter said. "I was just too slow to get it. It started here on the yacht. When we were first introduced, she hated my guts. Then all of a sudden she wants to dance and take me back to the fantail and parade her boobs. That was so that Feeyad could search my bag. Her moods as well. She's not as accomplished a thief as Boulda, and not a good actress."

Corliss snorted. "She acted for three years with Lloyd, the poor bastard."

"Yeah, she did. I'd guess the reason for that is that Lloyd had the money to give her what she wanted. At least until the scam came off and she could go back to Boulda and an even finer lifestyle."

The phone buzzed at Carter's elbow.

"Yeah?"

"We've got it, Nick, the whole bundle! And it's dynamite!"

"Better bring it down here," he told Chandra. "Let's keep all this between you, me, and Corliss."

"Two minutes," Chandra replied, and hung up.

"God, what a bitch," Corliss said.

"Yeah, she is that. She even set herself up the day of the snatch, said she had to have a drink. She probably called Veerdelph from that taverna by the pier and gave him the route we were going to take."

"Then the Italians headed back for Crotone, and Veerdelph drove her to Vólos. You think Feeyad is behind it all?"

The door swung aside and Chandra burst into the cabin.

"We'll soon know," Carter said.

Between the ledgers and the tape, they were able to piece together the financial tunnels and the hidden companies that made the whole thing go.

Feeyad had been investing deeply in Namibian mining and oil stock for years. It had paid off well, but not anything like it would pay off if there were some kind of guarantee that the South African government and South African companies would stay in control.

"So," Corliss said, "dump all your eggs in that basket and then go after the one thing—or person—who could put a monkey wrench in the works."

"Exactly," Chandra said, nodding. "Senator Samuel Lloyd. Get him to back off, and with enough money Feeyad could own Namibia."

"Chandra," Carter said, tapping the computer printouts, "is there enough here to prove collusion between Feeyad and Boulda?"

"More than enough," she replied. "In several cases Feeyad used funds from publically held companies. He siphoned the money through offshore banks into Aadlon. Then Aadlon invested even more heavily in Namibian stocks. It's all a house of cards."

"Which collapses if Lloyd gets his recommendation through," Carter murmured.

Chandra nodded. "There might still be enough to get indictments against all of them if it doesn't go through."

"Not good enough," Carter said.

"Why not?" Corliss asked.

The Killmaster turned to Chandra. "If Feeyad wins this squeeze play, how much will he be worth?"

She frowned in concentration. "Does the name J. Paul Getty ring a bell?"

"Yeah," Carter said.

"Imagine five times the worth, *after* taxes."

"There's your answer," Carter said. "Justice international is a fickle lady. If the pocketbook is bottomless enough, she can be swayed."

"Then we can't stop the bastards?" Chandra said.

"Let me think."

Carter paced the room for a full ten minutes, stopping now and then to stare out at the sea.

"Question," he said at last. "It's obvious that the Joanna Lloyd kidnap was a setup, a long-range plan to stop the senator. What they are doing now is stalling, keeping the senator here in Greece until after the crucial vote so he can't be where he should be to see it through."

"Agreed," Chandra said. "So?"

"What if we told him that?"

Corliss shook his head. "He would either not believe us, or, if he did, it wouldn't make any difference. He'd stick it out here and let the vote go to hell."

"Right on the nose, Bud old boy, right on the nose," Carter said. "Thought number two. What if I waltz in there and tell all, show the good Senator that his loving wife has made a patsy out of him, that she's actually married to another man, a thief and a con artist?"

Corliss and Chandra exchanged puzzled frowns. They both started to speak at once, but Carter held up his hand.

"We all know the answer to that. He'd snap like a twig. He's about ready to crumble anyway. If he learned the truth, he wouldn't be any good to himself or anyone else."

"Then what do we do?" Chandra said.

"Simple," Carter replied. "We give him back his loving wife."

EIGHTEEN

Carter stood on the roof of the old pickup truck. Bud Corliss was in the bed of the truck to his right. Both of them were dressed as farmers, in heavy work clothes with leather vests. Carter had a pair of binoculars to his eyes.

A half mile away was the villa registered in Hans Veerdelph's name, and, Carter was sure, financed by either Christopher Boulda or Zax Feeyad . . . or both. It was a sprawling, three-story affair perched on the very edge of a hundred-foot cliff. Around the villa, gardens, pool, and pool house, there was a massive stone wall.

The gate was a sheet of steel, the windows of the villa itself were tiny, and the men inside it would be armed. It was built of solid stone, and would withstand direct assault from anything less than a tank. The surrounding walls were of smooth stone, fourteen feet high, and, he could see when he climbed onto the truck's roof, wired for alarm bells.

Above the power line was barbed wire, held in position by steel angle irons, and in each of the angle irons was a photoelectric cell. Even from this distance, Carter could hear from inside the hum of a generator. It would do no good to try to cut off their power supply: they made their own, and guarded it.

The place was impregnable. Maybe. There was one long shot, and Carter decided to take it.

"Well?" Corliss asked.

"If I had the wings of an angel," Carter hummed, off-key, jumping to the ground and scrambling into the passenger seat. "Let's go."

Corliss drove the old truck down into the city of Vólos and on through. On the southern outskirts they stopped at a taverna and entered.

One of Damos's handsome, sturdy sons was in a booth with two giggly girls. He nodded as they passed. Carter nodded back and they took a booth in the rear. They ordered two beers and waited until they were served before they spoke.

"Well," Corliss said softly, "can you do it?"

"Get in, you mean?"

"Yeah."

"Oh, sure," Carter said, "I can get in. Getting out with her is going to be the problem. Especially if I have to carry her."

Damos's son slid into the booth. "How's tricks?" he said in English.

"Shitty," Carter replied in Greek. "What have you got?"

"The little one with the big chest?" he murmured, nodding toward the two girls in the booth. "Her papa takes food up to the villa every day. She goes with him."

"So," Corliss asked, "what are we looking at?"

"There is one womans and five mens," he said. "One of them is the big mans you described to me."

"Good," Carter said. "That means Feeyad is there. Did your father rent a boat?"

"Yes, a fine sturdy fishing caique. It is in the village of Ixos, near the mouth of the gulf."

Carter turned to Corliss. "You checked out Feeyad's plane?"

Corliss nodded. "It's a Lear, six passengers. You can't miss it. It's the only one at the Vólos airport."

"Okay," the Killmaster said, "here's what I'll need. Two muscle cars—and I mean *muscle*—something that will fly. I want 'em parked in back of that taverna at the bottom of the hill. I'll want two full magazines and an AR-17 in the one I use. Got that so far?"

Corliss nodded. "No problem."

"Also, I'll need climbing gear . . . ropes and suction cups. Petons would be too noisy. A four-prong grappling hook. Wrap the hook in rubber. Black shirt, black pants, dark sneakers, and lampblack for my face. Get me a waterproof bag with shoulder straps for the clothes."

"You swimming in?"

Carter nodded. "You saw those big spotlights on the back of the villa. If they turn those sweethearts on at night, they can see five hundred yards out into the gulf. Damos couldn't bring the caique in close enough to land me. That means I'll need a small rubber boat as well."

He dropped some bills on the table, and all three of them moved out into the harsh sunlight.

The boy looked up at the sky, sniffed, and chuckled. "I think you have good luck."

"How so?" Carter asked.

"Greek weather. Papa says by sundown we have rain."

• • •

Damos was a good forecaster. By dusk, dark clouds had rolled in from the sea. By nightfall it had started to rain, not hard, but steady. And there was no moon; not even a sliver scooted between the fast-moving clouds.

Carter dressed below and carried his gear up on deck. When he was set, he helped Damos take the big old caique out, the elderly diesel two-stroke clanking, coughing on a faulty cylinder. The hollow popping sound it made seemed unnaturally loud on the silent sea. The caique, like all caiques, was an unwieldy, primitive craft, broad in the beam, high in prow and stern.

They sailed out into the Aegean until the shore was no more than a smudge of darkness. Carter killed the engine and hoisted the creaking sail.

"When do we fish?" he asked.

"Later," said Damos. "Make for the gulf now. We'll pretend when we need to."

Carter obeyed, and the caique heeled over, eager for the breeze, the water chuckling, cackling past the old hard wood of the caique's bow.

For nearly an hour Carter stayed on course, almost due north, in the middle of the gulf. Then Damos came aft and took the tiller.

"There are the lights. I will stay to the south of them. Good luck."

Carter moved forward and squatted by the rail. When the caique hove to near the headland, he stared into the darkness, searching out the denser dark of cliff and villa. Then he stripped, piled his clothes into an inflated rubber raft, and lowered it into the water.

He murmured good-bye to Damos, then slipped silently into the calm, warm sea. Pushing the raft ahead of him, he swam toward the cliff, taking his time, cautious not to tire himself, until at last he reached pebbles, stood up, and dragged the raft onto a beach.

He took a towel from the raft, dried himself, and dressed. Then he deflated the raft and felt his way to the base of the cliff. Cautiously, he drew out a shaded flashlight and hid the raft at the foot of a rock. Then he looked along the cliff face, searching patiently until he found the alarm wire he knew must be there.

He climbed over it and, using the suction cups, started up the sheer rock wall. Halfway up, he found another alarm trip wire, and carefully worked his way over it. Near the very top he found yet another wire.

Then he was at the wall, smiling. He had guessed right. They hadn't expected any intrusion from the sea up a sheer rock cliff; the trip wires were the only gesture to defense from that quarter. There was no barbed wire on the wall, and the stone wasn't sensor-wired.

He cocked an ear for any sound from the other side, and heard nothing but music in the distance from inside the villa. He flipped the grappling hook, felt it find a purchase, pulled back until it held, and started up.

Again luck was with him. The giant lights on the rear of the house were off. The only lights at all were in the swimming pool, and that was far to his left.

He dropped to the ground in a maze of low trees and bushes. Like a predatory animal he crawled around until he found a soft spot to bury the line and grappling hook.

Carter moved forward and up onto the veranda. He kept low, beneath the windows, popping up now and then to take a look inside.

The first-floor rooms were vast and elegantly furnished, reminding him once more that Hans Veerdelph could never have afforded luxury like this.

Using the cups, he started up. In bedrooms on the second floor, two men slept. Neither of them was Boulda or Feeyad. Carter had a purchase with his toes on a narrow ledge, but he still used the suction cups as he moved along the rear of the house.

When he came to the lighted windows on the other side of the second floor, in the rear, he stopped and cautiously leaned around the sill and peered into the room.

It was a study, high-ceilinged, austere, yet it had a certain richness. Christopher Boulda and Zax Feeyad played chess at a small table near the fireplace. A third man stood by the table, watching. His white shirt had chevrons, and on his collar was a small pair of gold wings.

This, Carter thought, would be the pilot.

He backed away a few feet and headed on up to the third floor. Only one set of windows showed light. Gently Carter eased himself up to the iron railing of a balcony, and dropped softly to the tiles.

The wide French windows were open to allow the cool night breezes and the scent of the light rain into the room.

Carefully he eased out from the stone wall and looked into an enormous bedroom. To the right was a bathroom fit for a queen. An open door farther to the right revealed a walk-in closet crammed with clothes . . . expensive women's clothes. To the left was an enormous peachwood bed with a blue velvet canopy and coverlet.

And on the huge, canopied peachwood bed was a beautiful, lush-bodied blonde with long, showgirl legs, full breasts, and a petulant, sensual mouth glistening with freshly applied lipstick. She wore a low-cut lime-green dress of clinging silk. A long slit in the skirt reached far up one tanned leg. She dug the sharp stiletto heel of a black shoe deep into the velvet covering the bed and breathed shallowly as she buffed her nails and nodded her head in time with the music blaring from the radio.

Jane Preeva-Boulda, Joanna Frawley-Lloyd.

Carter flexed his right forearm and the stiletto, Hugo, slipped into his palm. With the silenced Luger in his left hand he stepped into the room.

"Nice digs, Jane. Or are you so used to Joanna that you don't answer to Jane anymore?"

The eyes went round, the mouth gaped, and she rolled to the side of the bed, her hand clawing for the night table.

In one lightning move, Carter flipped the stiletto, hilt to blade, in his palm. It made a singing sound going across the room and thudded into the headboard of the bed two inches from the woman's grasping fingers. The knife quivered there for seconds, and she couldn't seem to pull her eyes away from it until it stopped.

By that time Carter was at the side of the bed, standing above her. He curled his fingers in her blond hair and turned her face up to his.

"Wanna dance, lady?"

She tried to scream. It came out a hollow squeak as Carter slid his hand down and tightened his fingers around her neck. He brought her up to a sitting position and sat beside her on the bed, moving like a drowsy rattlesnake in the desert.

"You!" she gasped, her breasts rising and falling with her frightened breathing.

"Yeah, me," Carter hissed, his lips close to her ear. "You're going to do a little reading up on your friends. Then you're going to hear a little speech from me. Then we're getting out of here. Got it?"

Nothing.

He applied a little pressure behind her ears.

"Yes, yes, I hear!"

"Good, good, Jane-Joanna. Then we are going to talk, like the old friends we are. And when our little talk is over, you and me, we are getting out of here. Or I might just leave alone. And believe me, darlin', if it's only me goin' out all by myself, I am going to leave you very dead behind me."

NINETEEN

The brief that Amos Treadwell had worked up was almost two inches thick. Chandra had managed to pack it in a nice heavy cardboard folder. She had even wanted to title it "Manual for Thieves" on the outside, but Carter thought that a bit much.

As the woman read, he stood nearby, watching her. There was no need for threats now. The more she read, the less color remained in her face. Now and then she would look up with a comment.

"How did you get all this?"

"I'm a pretty good thief myself."

Back to reading she went, still angry, a tiny bit of bluff left in her manner.

"Hans never came back. Where is he?"

"Dead. Fish food," Carter replied.

That erased a little more of the cockiness. When she came to the end of the summation, she quickly flipped through the copies of the ledger and the printouts that Chandra and Ryder had pulled out of the computer concerning the shift of funds and its laundering.

By the time she dropped the whole thing to the bed, her entire body was shaking like a leaf.

It was then Carter knew he had her.

"I told Chris, right from the beginning, that it would never work," she murmured.

Carter crouched in front of her. There was no smile now, and he kept his eyes dead as he forced her to meet his gaze. When he spoke, it was through clenched teeth, without moving his lips.

"Right now, aboard the *Nobel Savage*, a few hundred of those dossiers are being made up. By midmorning tomorrow they will be in the hands of bankers, attorneys, Feeyad's investors, and the police of about nine countries."

"The stock . . ." she breathed.

"That's right," he growled. "I figure that by the time the Tokyo, New York, London, and Bonn exchanges close tomorrow, it will all be worthless. How much stock do you and Boulda have, Joanna?"

An answer would have been superfluous. It was on her face.

"Your sister, Hulda, and Nils Zefsheem down in Johannesburg? They might get off with twenty years. Boulda? It's hard to say. When they start digging on him, it could be life. Feeyad . . ."

Suddenly she smiled, a hollow, mocking smile. "Zax will never go to jail. He's got hidden funds. He'll go to Brazil or Argentina, where there's no extradition. He won't be able to live like a king anymore, but he'll live."

Carter shrugged. "Maybe, maybe not. And maybe he might be charitable enough to support your husband there . . . Boulda, I mean. But I doubt it. So that leaves you."

Her head had been hanging. Now it jerked up, the eyes flashing. "Me? What about me?"

"There's a grave in South Africa. The name on the stone is Jane Boulda. Who's in that grave?"

"I didn't kill her, I swear! It was Christopher. He strangled her in a hotel room."

"In Liberia?" Carter said.

"Yes."

"While you watched."

"I-I couldn't stop him."

"Who was she, really?" he growled, feeling the bile rise in his throat. This woman was as heartless as stone.

Joanna shrugged. "A French prostitute, no family. Chris checked her out."

"And then he paid some rummy doctor for a death certificate."

"Yes, but I didn't . . . I swear—"

The voice was suddenly on the edge of hysteria. Carter slapped her.

"Change clothes."

"What?"

"Put on some slacks, a sweater, clothes you can move in."

One corner of her mouth curved in an evil smile. The light slipped back into her eyes. "You're letting me go."

Carter stared at her, then slowly nodded. "In a way. Move."

She practically ran to the closet. When she started to close the door, he slammed it open.

"I don't want you coming up with any toys that go boom."

She glared at him for a few seconds, then slipped out of her dress and heels. Then she posed in lacy underwear.

"Enjoying the view?"

He appraised her openly, his gaze running up and down the voluptuous frame, the sensuous, womanly curves. Then his eyes met hers, icily. "Frankly, no. What you've got is too rich for my blood. It would make me sick."

She gave it up and started dressing. Carter talked.

"A friend of mine is going to drive you to the Athens airport. Senator Lloyd is waiting there with a chartered jet."

She paused, pulling on a sneaker. "Sam? I'm going back to Sam?"

"That's right," he said. "You're going to come through this frightful experience with flying colors. You'll cry a little. He'll comfort you. You'll tell him you don't want to talk about it right now. Maybe someday. For the next three or four days you'll stand beside him, the loving helpmate, while he gets that U.N. resolution passed."

She was dressed. "Then?"

"Then you're going to break down. You're going to admit you don't love him anymore. You're going to ask for a divorce."

"You're crazy!" she gasped.

"Like a fox," Carter replied. "It's going to hurt old Sam, but not half as much as this would have hurt him."

"But what happens to me?"

"I really don't give a shit what happens to you." He moved forward and laid the snout of the Luger's silencer across her neck. "Maybe you can join Boulda and Feeyad in Argentina or Brazil. One thing is for sure, Joanna . . . you're going to leave old Sam with just the clothes on your back."

"No way," she hissed.

"Wanna bet? Because, if you don't, I'm gonna show up again. And when I show up, accidents happen."

"You wouldn't dare!" She was shaking again now, badly.

"Your ass I wouldn't dare! I could scatter you in so many pieces over the landscape no one would even find a toe. You got it?"

She nodded, and Carter knew she meant it.

"Okay," he said, glancing around the room. "I'm told the Germans built this dump after the war. There are supposed to be ways in and out of here . . . some kind of a tunnel or something?"

For a moment she hesitated, then nodded. "Yes," she whispered.

"Show me."

She found a pad and pencil. Quickly she sketched a layout of the house.

"We're here," she said, pointing to the sketch, "on the third floor. The study is here, on the far end of the second floor, so they can't hear us."

"Where do these stairs go?"

"The kitchen. In back of the pantry, there's a door. Beyond the door there are stairs."

"That lead where?"

"Underground. They lead under the well. There's a well . . . here, about two hundred yards beyond the wall down the hill. The well is a phony. There are steps up to the top. The lid is locked from the inside."

"Neat," Carter growled, "very neat."

He pocketed the sketch and retrieved Hugo. The last thing he did before they left the room was prop the brief against one of her pillows.

"You're warning them?" she gasped.

Carter smiled. "Yeah. When does your con man husband usually join you?"

She looked at her watch. "In about an hour. They play chess every night until eleven."

"Let's go."

They left the room and tiptoed out into the hall. It was empty; a single light burned at the far end.

"We go this way," she whispered.

She led him down a dark passage that smelled of musty wood and dank stone. They came to the steps. The centers were worn into scoops after years of use.

Carter clicked on his penlight beam. It gave sufficient illumination to get them down to the floor below. They faced a second hall, on the ground floor. He raised his beam and swung it around.

"There's the kitchen."

They moved through the kitchen and into the pantry. Joanna ran her hand along the molding. There was a click and the wall popped forward an inch.

The stairs were wet and steep. Several times she slipped and cursed. Carter left her on her own. In the tunnel, they both had to move in a half-crouch.

They could hear scraping sounds all around them.

"What's that?" she cried.

"Rats," Carter said.

"Oh, my God . . ."

"Shut up. Move."

The well lid weighed a good two hundred pounds, but Carter managed to wrestle it open.

"This way down the hill to the taverna," he said, pushing her in front of him.

Twice she fell, and Carter yanked her up by the arm and pushed her on.

A pair of Mercedeses were in the parking lot behind the taverna. Bud Corliss and Damos's boy sat in the front seat of one of them.

"Here's your bundle," Carter said, shoving Joanna into the back seat. "The piece is in the other car?"

"Ready and waiting," Corliss said.

Carter leaned in through the window until his face was inches from the woman. "Remember what I said, Joanna, the loving wife. Then just the clothes. Any different and I'll find you." He slammed the door and stepped back. "Go!"

As soon as the taillights disappeared around the corner, he got in the second Mercedes.

He knew that even if Joanna had a thought right now about welching on her agreement, she would change her mind when she heard about Boulda and Feeyad.

Carter had parked the Mercedes in a thick grove of trees at the end of the single runway.

Now he lay near the fence, his eyes alert to the general area. There were four planes there. One of them was Feeyad's jet.

He had been waiting two hours.

Then they came, a big Citroën sedan. They drove within a few yards of the jet and piled out . . . Feeyad, Boulda, and the pilot.

Then Carter saw the big blue bird come trundling along the runway, taxi lights glowing, red rotating beacon flashing atop the vertical stabilizer, five-thousand-candlepower strobe on the belly shearing the night.

As the twin-engine jet came toward him, Carter watched. He needed no binoculars. With his exceptional eyesight and extraordinary night vision, he could see every detail; the pilot, Boulda in the right-hand seat, Zax Feeyad's bulk standing behind them.

Less than one hundred feet from him, Carter watched the jet slow, coming to a rocking halt, and wait while another airplane landed.

He heard the landing aircraft's tires squeal on impact, and a moment later Feeyad's jet moved forward again, its engines whining louder. It came to the end of the taxiway, steered around sideways toward Carter, then moved out toward the chevron-marked overrun end of the runway.

As the jet turned, Carter looked up the exhaust ends of both engines. It was like looking into hell . . . the spinning, fiery turbine blades that moved like orange discs rolling effortlessly through molten scarlet grease. Then the engines strobed, a sudden fiery flash without the slightest change in noise or power.

Carter sighted, lining the front sight up on the center of the left engine's spinning turbine. He took a breath, let half the air go, held clamping tight, centered the front-sight blade in the rear-sight aperture, and squeezed.

He put seven rounds into the left engine.

Let his breath go in a gasping snort.

Caught another deep breath, let half go, held on the right engine, and let off the remaining eight rounds.

Before he finished firing, the left engine self-destructed and then the right went, and Carter mentally complimented the instantaneous thinking and reaction of the pilot. He had both engines shut down almost the instant they began tearing apart.

But it was already too late. In seconds, flames had engulfed the fuselage.

Carter turned and raced to the Mercedes, cranking on the ignition and dropping it into gear. He floored the accelerator. He was flying, nearly a thousand yards from the jet, when the fuel tanks went.

The ground shock rocked the Mercedes, nearly jerking the wheel from Carter's hands. He managed to right the car, and stared into the rearview mirror.

All he could see was flames.

He wondered if enough parts of them could be found to identify.

He hoped so.

Damn, he thought, some holiday.

Then he looked on the bright side, and the thought brought a grin to his face.

There was Chandra, the *Noble Savage*, and a well-stocked bar.

DON'T MISS THE NEXT NEW
NICK CARTER SPY THRILLER

LAW OF THE LION

After a fast march of over an hour, Nick Carter reached the point on his grid maps where he believed the hospital setup of Dr. Charles Smith was located. Now he began fanning out in circles, looking for traces of road, utility lines or outbuildings for generators or propane gas containers.

The path, when he found it, was quite sophisticated, made of ground-up saplings and vines. It led Carter to a large building the size of an airplane hangar at a small airport, no great shakes in construction, but sturdy for the job. There were rib and truss beams forming an arc, mounted on top of a large square. Mounted on the outside of the large building were four large air conditioners. A quarter mile or so from the large building was a cinder-block building of about a hundred square feet. Carter had no trouble getting a look inside. His suspicions were confirmed: in it were three large generators and several drums of fuel.

There were only two signs on the large building, PRI-

VATE and NO UNAUTHORIZED ADMISSION. There were no indications of guards or campsites. As he circled closer, Carter did find a construction that convinced him Dr. Smith liked fresh flowers. A small greenhouse flourished in the tropical growth. Moving in for a closer look, Carter saw an interesting assortment of fuscias, begonias, and bright, cheery asters.

Poking closer to the main building, Carter got a look in a window and saw what was probably a nurse's quarters. At the next level of window, he saw what he had hoped to discover: a small room, well appointed with a hospital bed. Lying in the bed was a man whose face was swathed in bandages. Something familiar about the man tugged at Carter. It was Bud Gonder, the young student from the infirmary and the bomb explosion. Dr. Charles Smith apparently couldn't resist the challenge of giving people different appearances.

There were two other recovery rooms, but each was empty at the moment.

Carter did a quick tour around the building and saw nothing to spoil his earlier assessment about any kind of security system. He looked carefully for electronic alarms, found none, and decided he was going to take his chances by mounting the small four-step tier to the building and stepping inside.

He'd been in dozens of similar buildings, the walls painted in institutional colors and the lobby filled with regulation furniture. A series of doors led to small storage rooms, a nurse's lounge, and a small library with a computer hookup for data base research. A slightly larger door led to an impressive wood-paneled office about twenty feet square. There was a large mahogany desk, teak shelves, and a number of pre-Columbian artifacts. On the desk were several boxes of Cuban cigars. There were also a few large boxes of granola bars. Anticipating the hunger that would soon be on him, Carter took two bars.

Carter guessed this luxurious enclave was Dr. Charles Smith's office when he was in residence. It had the look, the smell, and the tone of a man who thought well of himself and wanted all his outward accouterments to reflect the fact.

Next to the office was a small, deluxe room with wood paneling, some first-rate graphics on the walls, a water bed, and an expensive stereo system with large, boxy speakers. Without spending too much time checking out meaningless details, Carter saw that there was a large modular shower and a full-length triple mirror. Dr. Smith traveled in style.

The thing Carter wanted to see next was down at the end of the hall, another large room, probably the same twenty-by-twenty dimension as Smith's office. This was the operating room, a first-class setup with a bank of overhead mercury vapor lamps, an adjustable table, long banks of X-ray readers, a huge autoclave for sterilizing instruments, a large wooden cabinet with several drawers and, finally, a huge glass cabinet filled with an array of knives, saws, drills, chisels, and other surgical tools. Lit by fluorescent wall fixtures for the times when the mercury vapors were not on, the room was a well-organized, efficient operating room.

Carter wondered if the Grinning Gaucho hadn't had his identity laundered in this very room.

The sound of nurses talking from a nearby room caused Carter to duck toward the door, but there he was met by the diminutive, cigar-smoking doctor, dressed now in stone-washed denims and running shoes. "The curiosity got to you, right?" he said.

Carter decided to tough it out by saying nothing.

"I can promise you, there will be little or no pain at

any time." He began to scan Carter's face. "It's a shame to do any work on a face like yours. You've got classic features. Good bones. Well, come on over here and let's get started."

"I think you have the wrong idea," Carter said.

The doctor became irate. "I think *you* have the wrong idea." He pulled the cigar from his mouth and heaved it forcefully. "Dammit, you'd think they'd do some kind of a briefing first." He stared at Carter. "You think I'm just going to sedate you and start cutting, right, fellow? Jeez, gimme a break. I take something like six hundred different measurements, some within a tenth of a millimeter. Then I build a topography—here, I'll show you." He moved to the large wooden cabinet and opened it, removing what looked to Carter like a death mask.

"It's called a moulage," the doctor said, extending a plaster cast toward Carter. "We're talking exquisite detail here, so don't go backing away like I was going to start cutting you right now. Hell, you can't know it, but you're getting the best. I give you features you'd never dream of." He studied Carter for a few moments. "I can fix it so your jaw will never pop again. You'll be free of that, you understand."

"Those casts are all of people you worked on?"

"Damned right," the doctor said. "That's just responsibility to keep track. Those bozos in the CIA are scared stiff someone is going to find my records and then everyone will recognize you." He snorted. "Hell, when I'm through with you, no one will recognize you."

Carter edged toward the door. "Thanks, but I think there's been a misunderstanding."

"I'm telling you," the doctor said, *"you're* doing the misunderstanding. I just want to measure you first.

Don't even think about surgery for a week or so. Now, be reasonable. Let's get on with the measurements."

Carter backed toward the door.

"That tears it," the doctor said. "Bruno! Marvin! I got a stubborn one here. Doesn't want to be measured."

The door opened and two men entered, both well over six four. One of them was black, his head shaven clean, a Puerto Vallarta T-shirt looking incongruous on his enormous frame. The other was a prototype of a wide receiver, blond, powerful, fast. They came at Carter. "Easy does it, buddy," the black guy said and extended his hand. "Doc here just wants to take some measurements with a small little ruler."

He feinted at Carter, who did not take the bait at all. "Let's cut this nonsense right now," Carter said.

"Hey, buddy, you let the doc measure you and we got no problems," the black guy said, reaching quickly for Carter and getting his hand. The Killmaster spun away, bumping the big blond off-balance. Carter danced back toward the black, elbowed him in the gut, and dropped into a crouch to take the charge from the blond.

Carter sidestepped that, tripped the blond, and was at the door. Both men were stunned with surprise. The black started at Carter again, driving him back against the blond, who got Carter in a bear hug, but Carter immediately shot his feet into the black guy's chest, dropping him and spinning away from the blond.

"I don't want to have to do this," Carter said.

The blond guy was out to save face. All seriousness now, he reached for Carter, who got a hand on the sleeve of his smock, tugged, and brought him to his knees with a crash. Frustrated, the blond got to his feet with some fancy gymnastics and came at Carter.

"What the hell is this?" the doctor shouted. "From

now on, they're all going to sign releases before they come to me. I've had it with this skittishness."

The blond threw a punch at Carter who caught it in his left hand, squeezed, twisted, and wrenched the man to the floor with a hard slam.

Carter was out of the room, down the steps, and out into the jungle as quickly as possible, the irate voice of Dr. Charles Smith bawling at the two goons.

Using his copy of the Mossad map, Carter oriented himself and set off at an angle across the vast expanse of jungle on the far side of the Center for the Arts. He moved at a fast pace for nearly an hour before he paused for a cigarette.

—From LAW OF THE LION
A New Nick Carter Spy Thriller
From Jove in August 1989